BACK AWAY

FROM THE SHOES

By

MILA A. BALLENTINE

PUBLISHER'S NOTE
This novel is a work of fiction told from the perspective of fictitious character experiences. The names, places and characters are products of the author's imagination. Any resemblance to actual persons living or dead, business establishments, event or locals is coincidental.

CHAPTER ONE

Danish architecture highlighted the coastal suburb where middle class families thrived and a few empty nesters enjoyed the tranquility. Homeowners obsessively mowed their lawns and hired landscapers to maintain a picturesque curb appeal. Hedges were fashioned into topiary animals or symbols depending on the homeowner's personality. Their efforts raised property values and set them apart from neighboring communities. Everything was dandy in Paradise Falls, Maine.

Topiary peacocks decorated the edge of the lawn and cherubs guarded the cobblestone walkway that led to the Sullivan's front door. Pink and red rose bushes stood against the banana-yellow house covered with a red roof and hunter-green decorative shutters. Dew settled on their lawn and mist filled the edges of Casey's window. The sunlight invaded the room and her eyes opened as the alarm clock sounded. She crawled out of the covers, and yawned. Casey passed her hand through her hair and went to the bathroom. She returned to her room and stood in front of her closet.

Her father spent the past month renovating it. Adam built a dresser in the center. Shoe racks lined the wall above the dresser and below the clothing racks on each side. Casey parted the clothes on the rack; the elevated shoe racks displayed flats, wedges, and heels in every color. It was easy to find a particular shoe but hard to decide which pair to wear. Casey walked away from the closet and sat on the edge of the bed. She couldn't think straight. She had to find the perfect shoes, but not today.

Casey went back to the closet, closed her eyes and chose a pair of shoes. She looked at the mirror on the closet door, and turned to the side. Her green eyes added depth to the luminous black hair that cascaded off her shoulder. She corrected her posture to get a prime view of the red blazer over a blue and white striped shirt and a blue pleated skirt. She stepped back, flexed her slender calf sideways, and looked at the black suede lace-up wedges on her feet. *Not bad.*

"Casey, it's time to go. I don't have all day," her mother, Kelly, shouted from the bottom of the spiral staircase.

"I'll be right down." Casey grabbed her bag and went downstairs.

"I can't afford to be late." Kelly looked at her watch, "we're working on a big project." She looked in the hall mirror, fixed a strand of her light brown hair that escaped her ponytail and applied mascara. Kelly tamed her long eyelashes, bringing out her intense blue eyes, and her tailored eyebrows made her eyes look fuller.

Adam passed them in the hall in his pajamas, opened the front door, and picked up the newspaper. He went into the kitchen, made himself a cup of coffee, sat down and opened the newspaper. Kelly walked out the side door into the garage.

"Hey where's my kiss?" Adam asked.

4

"Adam!" It was hard to say no once she looked into his brown eyes. Her hand fingered his dark brown hair.

"A kiss only takes a second." He puckered his lips above his masculine jaw line.

Kelly kissed him; he lingered there for more than a second and wrapped his broad muscular arms around her torso. Casey cringed and got in the car.

"Love you," he said before Kelly entered the car and drove away.

Casey forgot to put on makeup, but she had a backup stash in her bag. She tried to put on eyeliner and mascara while her mother fussed about drivers who traveled at Sunday speed. Kelly passed cars like the plague if they weren't going at or above the speed limit. As long as her mother stayed clear of potholes, she managed to get her makeup on.

Her mom pulled up in front of Central High School. The light-gray two-story brick fortress with massive windows and manicured lawns made the school look like an open environment, but it was an illusion. Once a student was inside, *rules* ruled.

"Thanks. Drive safely," Casey said before her mother drove away.

Her best friend sat on the picnic table under a large tree on the front lawn. They had been friends since primary school. Francesca was new to their elementary school, when Casey befriended her, but some of the kids gave her a hard time. One student said, "There are too many black people in our school." His comment was weird because there were only five African American students in the entire school. Francesca held her own and never let comments like those faze her, and Casey admired her strength.

Francesca's natural honey-tanned skin, hazel-green eyes, and an easy smile made her stand out from the rest of the white students that littered the lawn. Casey walked over and sat next to her.

"I like your outfit. How did you come up with it?" Francesca asked.

"When I'm asleep I envision myself sorting through my closet and I make a decision."

Francesca burst out laughing, "Are you serious, or are you kidding me?"

"Yes, I'm serious and no, I'm not kidding," she said.

"Well whatever you're doing, it's working." Francesca had to admit, her friend had a knack for fashion.

Casey had a fondness for shoes and fashion, but solving mysteries intrigued her, and it fueled her desire to pursue a career in law enforcement. Being a part of her school's Law Enforcement and Public Safety Program was encouraging. Each student enrolled in the program was required to immerse themselves in extracurricular activities related to the field. Unlike most of her peers, she worked part time after school, and working at the Reinhold Detective Agency was the perfect fit. When the last bell rang, it was her cue to gather her things as quickly as possible so she wouldn't be late for work.

Casey sat at her desk and aimlessly flipped through the open case files, Mr. Reinhold left on her desk the day before, when the phone rang.

"Reinhold Detective Agency, Casey speaking."

"Is Mr. Reinhold in?" he said.

"He's not in at the moment. Would you like to leave a message?"

"Sure, tell him Buddy called."

Casey loved working as a receptionist at the detective agency. The type of clients her boss took on was a coin toss. From the moment a client entered, she guesstimated what their case was about, and nine times out of ten, she was right. When it turned out a husband had cheated, the wife broke down and Mr. Reinhold consoled her. Within a few days, the jilted wife was his intimate sidekick until a new client came along.

Casey didn't understand what his clients saw in him. His best assets were his earthy green eyes and the ability to talk his way in or out of any situation. Shaving scars warped his cheeks, a thick mustache hugged his almost nonexistent lip, graying eyebrows and a side-part in his dark wavy hair made him a dapper implant from an era before her time.

There were times when the office was quiet to the point that it encouraged insanity. Casey stayed sane by flipping through the entourage of women's magazine subscriptions Mr. Reinhold received. She sifted through the titles, People, Glamour, Conde Nast Traveler, and Essence magazine. Her eyes lit up when she saw the new addition to his collection, Teen Vogue. Casey looked at the clock on the wall. He was usually here by this time of the day.

She got up, locked the front door and went to the bathroom. While inside, she heard Mr. Reinhold's keys jingle when he opened the door. She washed her hands and left the bathroom. Their eyes met as she closed the door behind her. A thick coat of blood streamed from his nose and his right eye was bloodshot.

"Are you okay?" Casey rushed towards him.

"Whoa! It's not a big deal." Mr. Reinhold retrieved a handkerchief from his pocket and wiped the blood. It looked like 'a big deal' to her. Mr. Reinhold's face looked like he accidentally ran into a parked fist and was the unfortunate one to get a ticket. He said he was fine, so she went back to her desk, but her eyes followed him until he entered and closed his office door.

CHAPTER TWO

Francesca siphoned moolatte out of a straw, while Casey window-shopped as they strolled through The Greenville Mall. They abandoned their listless stroll and looked down from the third level balcony. The mall patrons looked like stray sheep. The higher the sale percentage, the more likely they were to graze.

"It's a good size crowd today." Francesca slurped the last ounce of moolatte before she tossed it in the trash.

"As long as money exists, there will always be people at the mall," Casey said and laughed.

"Come on, let's get some Chinese food," Francesca said.

They went down to the first level. There were various oriental restaurants.

"Let's go to the Golden Nugget," Francesca said.

They walked to the end of the food court. The Golden Nugget was one of the smallest restaurants, but they had the most customers. The line formed an elongated L around the common dining area. Ten minutes went by. Francesca took off her heels and they dangled from the tips of her fingers. Casey rested her hands on the counter. Francesca's curly black hair bounced with the slightest move she made. The black and white striped shirt she wore hung off her shoulder. She turned to Casey, "what are you having?"

"The same thing you're having."

Francesca turned her attention to the young man dressed in white behind the counter. His eyes were primed on the pad in his hand.

"Can I take your order please?"

"Two orders of curry wings with vegetable fried rice and two ice teas."

He turned toward the kitchen and spoke to the cook in Chinese. Casey and Francesca stepped away from the counter and stood off to the side. Ten minutes later, Casey sighed, "Gosh, I'm starving."

"No you're not! Children in Africa are starving. You're hungry," Francesca said.

"Whatever." Casey rolled her eyes from one end to the other. Her attention turned to the people waiting in line. The hair on Casey's neck stood up. She felt like a lone fruit at the top of a tree with a group of hungry people waiting below to devour her. Francesca paid no attention to their stares. She didn't walk to the mall barefoot. Her feet hurt, and that was all the justification she needed to take her shoes off.

"Francesca!" the young man at the counter said and placed the tray of food in front of them. He said her name so fast it sounded like he strangled each syllable and Francesca jerked to attention. Casey took the order, while Francesca paused and knelt to put on her black patent high heels. A warm light bounced off the side of her legs as she fastened the strap on her shoes. Casey walked toward the seating area and when she realized Francesca wasn't beside her, she looked back.

The line at the Golden Nugget regenerated. The line went on forever and Francesca was the sideshow. Her beauty was undeniable; her complexion was a compilation of caramel with a hint of molasses. She caught up with Casey and they sat down.

"So have you found a pair of shoes for the prom yet?" Casey asked.

Francesca glared at her, "I don't have time to worry about that! I'm focused on more important matters, like passing Algebra."

"Oh that's nothing, I can help you with that," Casey bit into a curry wing and her taste buds did the 'river dance.' "It's delicious."

"I see why the line is so long. Their food makes your tongue give your hands a high-five." Francesca laughed aloud, "You're hilarious."

Casey didn't say another word until she finished eating.

"Where do we go from here?" Casey slouched in her chair.

"For starters, we're going to walk off some of this food before it sticks to our thighs," Francesca said.

"Come on let's go." Casey emptied their trays and stacked them above the other trays. They got on the escalator, got off on the second level, and walked inside *Forever 21*.

"Can I help you find anything?" a sales associate popped out of a corner like a jack-in-the-box, startling Francesca.

"No," Casey said before they walked away from her. Groups of girls from their high school were inside the store. One of the girls waved at Francesca.

"Who's that?" Casey hadn't seen her before.

"That's Sissy. She's nuttier than squirrel shit but she's okay," Francesca said.

Casey laughed. Francesca went over to the accessory rack attached to the wall. She tried on a few bracelets and put earrings against her ear.

"Did you find anything you like?" Francesca asked. Casey was over at another accessory rack.

"No." She walked over to the register and stood next to Francesca. The cashier gave Casey a bag with her items and they left the store.

"I don't know about you, but I'm tired," Casey said and a yawn escaped her mouth.

CHAPTER THREE

Randy ran into her room, clawed his way onto her bed, and lay next to her. His hot breath hovered just below her nose. Her eyes twitched, nose wiggled, and face grimaced while she slept. Casey opened her eyes to see her ten-year-old brothers' pug. Randy's bulging eyes stared at her and his 'funky-town' breath made her shudder. His shiny brown coat glistened as the sun shone through an opening in the curtains. He turned his head sideways. Randy reminded her of a waterlogged prune.

"Henry! Get him out of my room!"

Henry shuffled down the hall and into her room. His pale-blue eyes were always the first thing that caught her attention. His curly blonde hair and eyebrows matched his complexion and made it look like he didn't have any eyebrows at all. When he smiled, he displayed a chipped tooth he inherited a month earlier. Henry had taken Randy for a walk and Randy took off when he saw a squirrel. Henry fell and hit his chin on the sidewalk trying to catch him, thus chipping his tooth.

"What are you waiting for?"

Henry frowned and gave Casey a death stare, not budging. They stared at one another until he finally blinked.

"Ha! I won. Now get Randy out of my room."

He came closer and tugged on Randy's spiked collar

and the pug jumped off the bed and stood next to his foot. Henry stuck his tongue out, saliva gurgled under his tongue. Casey sighed heavily and sat up in bed.

"You know what they say…after a while people start to look like their dogs; good luck Henry."

Randy growled at her and Henry narrowed his eyes before he walked through the door and slammed it. Casey fell back on her pillow and pulled the covers over her head. She went back to sleep for a few hours before she woke up and went down stairs. Her mother was in the kitchen.

"I was about to check to see if you were alive."

"'Damien' and his hell-hound woke me but I managed to go back to sleep." Casey opened the refrigerator door, looked around and then closed it.

Kelly smirked, "His name is Henry."

"If you say so, but I think he's an evil spawn."

"We're going on a date and I need you to keep an eye on your brother while we're out."

"Aww, mom you're killing me. Can't you get a babysitter?"

"Of course, it's you."

Blood pooled in Casey's cheeks. "Fine, I'll watch him, but if he's not breathing when you get home it's your fault." She grabbed an apple out of the fruit bowl and bit into it.

"Henry will be fine." Kelly hugged Casey and kissed her on the forehead.

It was the curse of being the eldest. It was hard to avoid the responsibility of taking care of a younger sibling. Henry had the ability to get under her skin. She hoped this wouldn't be one of those occasions. Casey looked out the window as her parents pulled out of the driveway, and her freedom left with them. For the next two hours, she was stuck with Henry whether she liked it or not. Her frown turned into a devilish grin.

"Henry!" She listened; his feet pattered on the hardwood floor.

"What?" Henry answered with a hint of disdain from the end of the hall.

"Would you like to watch a movie?"

"Sure," he responded enthusiastically.

The time Casey's parents were away was going better than she expected. Once she put on the movie, Henry was on his best behavior. He was in his own private movie theater and Casey was his server. A large bowl of popcorn, a box of red-hot's and a glass of ice tea were within arm's reach. If it were his last hour on earth, he would die happy.

"I'm going to make a phone call," Casey said before she left the room. The previews played. Then the screen went black and displayed a white ring with the title. Casey peeked from the corner of the hallway that separated the living room before going up the stairs. She spoke with Francesca for the next 20 minutes over the phone.

"Aren't you babysitting Henry?" Francesca hoped she hadn't taken up too much of her time.

"Yes, but I pacified him."

"What's that supposed to mean?"

"He likes movies, so I put one on for him to watch."

"That was nice of you, but for some reason, I think you're leaving something out."

"I put *The Ring* on for him to watch."

The phone went silent for a few minutes before Francesca spoke.

"Poor Henry, that movie scared the crap out of me. I couldn't sleep with the closet open for months. I kept seeing the girl with long black hair opening her mouth and meowing. You should check on him."

"Okay, hold on." Casey went downstairs, an empty red-hot box littered the center table and an empty bowl were the only hints left of Henry's private party. He was lying curled up on the couch. Casey walked over and knelt beside him.

"Henry," she asked him, noticing that his eyes were red. "What's wrong?"

"I'm scared and I have to pee."

The muscles in her face tensed, "Francesca, I have to go. I'll call you later." Henry burst into tears and clung to her, wrapped his legs around her waist and hands around her neck.

"You're choking me," Casey gasped and Henry eased up on his grip.

She took him to the bathroom. "Go," she said, but he didn't budge. It was the first time she had done something to him that she regretted. Henry didn't deserve this.

"Okay, I'll go in with you."

"No! I don't want you looking at me." Henry folded his arms, and if his lip got any longer, it would touch his chin.

"I'll go in the shower and keep the curtains closed." Henry thought about her suggestion for a moment.

"Okay, but no peaking!"

She stepped into the shower and closed the curtain. Casey was able to calm Henry before her parents got home, but guilt clung to her flesh like skunk musk. Perhaps going to work would cure those feelings.

CHAPTER FOUR

Casey returned from her lunch break and opened the door. Mr. Reinhold came out of his office at the same time she walked in the door and he jerked to attention.

"It's just me." She could see the relief on his face.

"Are you in some sort of trouble Mr. Reinhold?"

"No." He walked over to her desk and put a few files on the desk. She was young but she knew a lie when she heard it. *Suit yourself,* she thought. *When they scrape you off the sidewalk, you'll be singing a different tune.*

Casey went over to her desk and sat down. The hot sun hit her back through the open blinds and rendered the air conditioning useless. Beads of sweat ran down the length of her back. It got to the point where she couldn't take much more. Casey got up, closed the blinds, and turned around.

Outside, a woman stepped out of her BMW 335si convertible and looked up at the sign that hung from the two-story brownstone building. The Reinhold Detective Agency's building was narrow compared to the others. One could imagine the owner lost the fight in the land wars and the building had been squeezed into submission by the larger buildings on the block.

What the building lacked on the outside, it made up for on the interior. The woman felt like she was walking down a fashion runway, minus the succession of flashes from a photographer's lens. She was immaculately dressed in a white business suit as she stood in front of the doorway. Casey looked at her shoes that were highlighted by the sunlight.

"Welcome to The Reinhold Detective Agency, how can I help you?" Casey asked. The woman's blonde shoulder-length wavy hair hid one side of her face. She walked toward Casey, pulled off her red satin gloves and held them in her long fingers.

"You know, it's important to pay utilities; they are essential for a business. It is hot in here." She ran her index finger along the Rosewood accent table that held the silk flowers. She looked at the dirt on her hand and dusted it off. Her stiletto tapped the floor sending a Morse code to Mr. Reinhold. His ears perked...*we have company*.

Casey laughed, "They're paid! I just closed the blinds. Have a seat, please." Casey got up and opened the blinds behind her. The light invaded the room and the woman in white shielded her eyes.

Mr. Reinhold emerged from his cave with a cigar jammed in the corner of his mouth.

"So, what can we do for you?"
Smoke hovered around his face, and the aroma trickled around the office. He walked over to the desk and passed his hands over his hair then put his hands

in his pockets. The woman glanced at him, pursed her red lips in his direction and raised her eyebrows.

Casey looked at Mr. Reinhold. He was in 'case mode.' When he got that way, he was all tough, no fluff. Her attention shifted to the woman in white. Mr. Reinhold extended his hand, "I'm Thomas Reinhold. What mystery can I solve for you?"

The woman sat down and crossed her mile-long legs. Her stiletto shoes were on full display.

"Orli Rothman." She shook his hand. "It's a delicate matter." She got up and walked over to the window, tipped a blind and peaked outside, "and it requires the strictest confidentiality."

"It's the only way we do business. Come into my office so we can discuss it further."

Mrs. Rothman walked inside.

"Hold my calls," he told Casey as he closed the door.

His cases lately lacked luster, but by looking at the size of the diamond wedding band on her finger, Prada bag and shoes, Mrs. Rothman's dilemma could potentially hold its weight in gold for his business.

CHAPTER FIVE

Mr. Reinhold paced around the office. His black suspenders stood out against the white dress shirt. He was on edge more than usual. The phone rang and Casey answered it. The person on the other line said nothing, but heavy breathing resonated before Casey hung up.

"I'll need Mrs. Rothman's file before you leave for the day."

"Sure." Casey retrieved the file from the file cabinet. She had never seen him so invested in a case and it heightened her curiosity.

"So, what's this case about?" She placed the file in his hand.

"I'd like to tell you, but if I do I'd have to kill you."

"Kill me." Casey was determined to find out.

"Sorry Kiddo, this one is above your pay grade." His comment bothered her, but she managed to keep a straight face.

"Fine." She looked at her watch. "I have to go. I'm meeting with Francesca." Casey got her bag and left the office.

She arrived at the mall and waited for Francesca in the common eating area across from the Golden Nugget. She looked at her watch. The Food Court was filled with customers refueling after a shopping spree. Francesca was always on time. Ten minutes went by before she saw her hurrying to the eating area.

"Hi, sorry I'm late," she said out of breath. "There was an accident just off the main street on my block. Instead of drivers driving so everyone could get to wherever they were going, they slowed down to see what was going on, and slowed traffic in the process."

"It's okay," Casey sighed. "So how have you been?"

"Good, but I missed you."

"Me too," Casey said.

"Okay, enough of the mushy stuff."

"I'm going to get something to eat from the Golden Nugget. Do you want anything?" Casey got up from the table.

She walked up to the counter. One of the workers from the Golden Nugget came out to the eating area to retrieve trays for their customers. He came over to the garbage bin directly behind Francesca. A loud crash echoed behind her and she turned around to see a young man dressed in white. When he picked up the trays off the floor, their eyes met. She smiled and turned around. He put the trays on the counter and returned with a broom and dustpan to clean up the remnants of food scattered on the floor.

"Francesca," he said in a familiar compacted way. She turned around abruptly.

"Yes?" She glanced at him, wondering how he knew her name.

He wiped his hands on the apron wrapped around his waist. He put his hand on his chest, "I'm Nu Gin from your science class."

She noticed his thin eyebrows and shy smile. The name sounded familiar, but he didn't look familiar. He took off his hat and she saw his jet-black spiked hair.

"Oh! Yes, I've seen you before."

"We were science partners in the sixth grade," Nu said.

Francesca smiled, "That was a long time ago. I don't even remember what happened last week."

"It was nice seeing you again, but I have to get back to work," he said and walked away.

Casey came back to the table after Nu left.

"Who was that?"

"Someone from school, let's eat."

CHAPTER SIX

A fork full of scrambled eggs entered Casey's mouth. Henry swirled his scrambled eggs around in the melted butter that settled on his plate. Casey felt someone's cold feet brush against hers. Her mother sat next to her, fully engaged in a text-a-thon with her assistant. A brush of the foot turned into footsies. Her father was on the other side of the table trying to get his wife's attention. Casey looked under the table and rolled her eyes.

"Dad, quit playing with my feet." Casey got up from the table. Kelly's eyes never left the screen of her cell phone.

"Sorry, I thought—."

"Don't! Dad!" She squinted her eyes and dropped her fork.

"Mom, are you taking me to school today?" Kelly didn't answer.

"I'll take her." Adam got up from the table and grabbed his keys off the counter.

She liked it better when her mom took her to school. When her dad did, he talked the entire time. *How is work, school, and the universe? Blah, Blah, Blah!*

"Okay, but no questions Dad."

Adam laughed, "Sure, I can do that."

He kept his word but it made the ride to school awkward. She hoped that the day would improve.

Somehow, Mrs. Phillips class ensured the opposite. Casey could tolerate any class at school except her second period class. On the first day of school, she was the last student to enter the class and got stuck with the seat directly in front of the teacher. Casey entered the room and sat at her desk.

"Casey, I'd like you to hand out the homework assignment," Mrs. Phillips said.

Casey distributed the papers to the class. Mrs. Phillips stood in front of the blackboard and erased the writing from the day before. Today her hair was straight and flowed down to her waist. Last week it was curly and stopped just above her neck. Either Mrs. Phillips had hair that grew faster than the average human hair, or it was a wig. One thing Casey knew for sure was that Mrs. Phillips knew how to accessorize her flawless outfits. Everything matched; even the nail polish.

There were advantages of sitting in front of a teacher; she could see the chicken scratches Mrs. Phillips wrote on the board, while the other students squinted and asked the student next to them what a word was. The downside was that she had to be on her best behavior and that she sat in front of Clarissa Vaughn. She was slender and one of the tallest girls in school. Students secretly called her *Big Bird* but none dared to say it to her face. Clarissa wore beanies every day, even in the summer.

She kicked the back of Casey's shoes for the better part of class. Casey liked her shoes more than she liked Clarissa. When Clarissa got tired of abusing Casey's shoes, she kicked the tray beneath Casey's seat. The metal sang with each kick. Casey stood up, and turned around. Clarissa's light brown hair cascaded in layers around high cheekbones and hollow cheeks.

"STOP!" Casey's mouth was so wide they could see her tonsils.

Mrs. Phillips spilled her coffee on her notes. All the air seemed to leave the room. The room went silent.

"Okay, settle down." She cleaned up the coffee with a handful of napkins. Casey eased back into the chair, but her face had gone from pink to blood red. Mrs. Phillips continued with the lesson and Casey tried to regain composure when another *tap* vibrated beneath her. The bell rang, preventing her from losing her cool. She gathered her books and walked into the crowded hall.

Casey glared at Clarissa and her friends as the congregated in the hall outside of Mrs. Phillips Class. Clarissa was a bother, but over the past few months, she had gained a following that kept growing. Brandy, a dough-faced wannabe socialite with deep-set blue eyes and blonde hair, was Clarissa's right hand. It was a feat, but she managed to date half the football team. Kim was a star player on the girls' basketball team. Her slender frame coupled with double D-breasts made her look older. And Lauren, a stone-faced chick with thick eyebrows and a quirky smile joined the crew by default. Her olive complexion, long black hair that rested on her broad shoulders and the bright clothing she wore screamed for attention. One day after school, Clarissa's car wouldn't start. Lauren, who had been relaxing under a tree walked over.

"What's wrong with your car?"

Clarissa tried to start the car again. Lauren noticed that no lights displayed on the dashboard.

"It's your battery. Pop the hood." Lauren advised and Clarissa pulled the lever. Lauren removed the terminal, cleaned the heads of the battery and put the terminal back on. This time the car started. Clarissa was impressed. Lauren was her spare tire ever since. Casey brushed past Clarissa and her crew and walked through the crowd of students. She went into the lunchroom. Today's special was a slimy chicken sandwich or undercooked pizza; neither appealed to her. She left the lunchroom and stood by the see-through panels on the side of the glass doors.

Casey looked out at the courtyard.

"Hi Casey, what's wrong? You look like you're contemplating warfare," Francesca said.

"Not quite, but anything is possible." Clarissa had ruffled her feathers and her angst was visible.

"Don't let it ruin your day," Francesca said.

The tree above them swayed and released a cool breeze. Francesca exhaled. "Is anything interesting going on at work?"

"I'm sorry to disappoint you, but we haven't had any cheaters in over a month," Casey said.

"Wow, I guess they're learning what not to do from the Maury and Jerry Springer shows."

Casey laughed, "No, they learn how to be more deceptive."

"We're working on a top-secret case and I'm in the dark."

"You could always take a look at the file," Francesca hinted.

"I thought about it, but I couldn't look him in the eye if I did. But I can look her up online."

Later that day, Casey googled Orli Rothman and a lot of information came up. Orli came to the US as a Norwegian foreign exchange student. She fell in love and married a wealthy oil executive. Mrs. Rothman was involved in numerous charities and was on the board of directors of a few of them.

While on vacation with her husband in Germany, they were involved in an automobile accident on the Autobahn. Driving on the Autobahn was a liberating feeling, compared to the speed limits in America. On the autobahn, the one-hundred mile-per-hour speed limit was a line between life and death. Unfortunately, that line was thinner than they had hoped. Her husband died in the crash. Orli was seriously hurt. Doctors' decided that an induced coma would improve her chances. Once she came out of a coma, months of intense physical therapy followed.

Orli Rothmans' strut was effortless; it was hard to tell that she had been in a debilitating accident. She was unbearable at times, but she was a survivor.

CHAPTER SEVEN

A lot was going on in Casey's life, and for a while, she had forgotten about finding a pair of shoes for the prom. Casey decided to visit the shops downtown. Each building had a distinct architectural personality, and the edges of the buildings met seamlessly, even though the colors varied from pastel to neutral colors. There were many stores from which to choose. Some catered to an older crowd while others catered to younger clients. In the end, the style and taste of the customer was the deciding factor.

Casey wasn't sure what type of shoes she was looking for. Francesca was supposed to meet her downtown, but canceled at the last moment. It was okay, she could handle finding the perfect shoes, if she could deal with Mr. Reinhold's eccentric clients. Her eyes traveled the store fronts, noticing that most of the shoes in the display windows looked like something an older person would wear to church or to a funeral. Casey sighed, *what does a girl have to do to find the perfect shoes...kill someone?*

She was just about to give up when she approached a quaint boutique on the corner of Delancey Drive. A modest sign with the name *Killer Shoes* hung above the entrance. Casey smiled; she found a hidden gem and went in. The flame of a Merlot candle danced as a light breeze came inside, invading the controlled environment. It smelled earthy and enhanced her desire to get to know the store more intimately.

A marble faux fireplace graced the north wall and a large gold ornate frame mirror hung above the fireplace. A large Tiffany vase filled with pastel colored silk flowers stood on the mantel of the fireplace. A young woman with lilac hair and a pale complexion stepped out into her gaze.

"It's a lovely day for shopping." She was a vision of perfection dressed in a silk long-sleeve short dress with an assortment of gold, peach and gray sequins in a floral design, with peach heels.

"Yes it is." Casey looked around the store. "How long have you been here?" she asked.

"We've been open a year."

"I've never heard of this store."

"We were on the front page of the Tribune. Killer Shoes was voted one of the best stores downtown," she said enthusiastically.

"I'm in the right place then." Casey's eyes lit up.

"What occasion are you shopping for?"

"The prom. I'm looking for the *perfect* shoes."

"That's code for 'nothing else will do'." She smiled and nodded her head.

Casey laughed, "Yup!"

"We have a large collection. My name is Lynn. Let me know what size you need when you decide."

Casey took her time looking at the wall-to-wall display of cascading shoes with designer brands on one side and the inspired by designs on the other. There was no attempt by the creator to imitate details of a designer brand but there were vague similarities. Casey wasn't naïve; she knew she couldn't afford designer shoes. It would take a year of her salary to afford one pair. Besides, there were more important things in life than wearing a mortgage payment or car note on her feet.

Casey's mouth watered. She sorted through the designer shoes and made a few selections.

"I'd like these in a size 7 ½ please."
Casey held three pairs. Lynn looked underneath the sole on the label. "We have these two in your size, but none in this style," Lynn said before she went to the stock room. She returned a short time later.

"Here yah go." She placed the boxes on the chair next to Casey.

Casey took each pair for a walk around the store and posed in front of the mirror for the final seal of approval. She was just 'keeping up with appearances'. Casey didn't have designer money but that didn't mean she couldn't try on designer shoes. She took off the shoes and put the others in the boxes.

"They're cute, but the fit's not right," Casey said, and gave the shoes to Lynn.

"I'm sure you'll find something." Lynn placed the boxes behind the counter.

Casey moved on to the inspired by collection and that was when the adventure turned productive. It was easy to have fun when it came to her weakness...shoes. She had been there for over an hour. The music playing made time pass without her realizing it. The store's choice of music was deliberate. Elevator music wasn't allowed. They put on music with an upbeat tempo to make the customer want to break into a dance. Then patrons would sign their entire check over to the business before curtsying and dancing out the door. *Goodbye money, hello heartache*.

The way things were going, Casey would close the store with Lynn. She still hadn't found what she was looking for. She couldn't decide. All of the shoes were undeniably beautiful.

After much deliberation, Casey found them. A pale pink shoe with a glass heel, straps crossed over the top of the feet with satin roses and pink cubic zirconium in the center.

"Do you have this in a seven and a-half?"

Lynn looked underneath the shoe, "yes we do." Casey wiggled with excitement when she left the room.

"Here you go." Casey removed the shoe from the box and took them for a spin around the store.

"I found them, the perfect shoes." She took the shoes off, put them in the box, and walked over to the register. Lynn happily typed in the total on the register.

"That will be two-hundred seventy-five dollars. Would you like to donate a dollar to the Bedford home for children?"

"Sure." Casey gave her the cash and Lynn put the box in a bag.

The door swung open, and a brisk breeze entered. The Merlot candle's flame died and a smoky odor persisted. Lynn and Casey's attention turned to the front door. Three masked men stood inside the front door dressed in black; their entire bodies were covered in sophisticated paintball apparel. Black thermal paintball goggles with colored lenses clung to their faces. The door retracted and closed. One of them flipped the open sign over to 'closed' and locked the manual clip above the dead bolt lock. Another walked over to them, lifted his hand and displayed the muzzle of his gun.

"Don't try anything or I'll have to hurt you." He spoke through the vent in the mouth guard. His voice sounded unrealistic, as if he were trying to talk under water. The other two men stood on opposite sides of the store, one as a lookout and the other as a backup in case anyone tried to be a hero.

Casey's legs froze in place. *Breathe and you will make it through this in one piece.* Lynn tried to remain calm, but she was falling apart at the seams. Her teeth began to chatter and she rubbed her hands together repeatedly.

"Cut that shit out, your making me nervous. Keep your hands where I can see them," the gunman shouted and waved the gun.

Lynn and Casey stood there like two stray cats caught in a box.

"I want a size ten, eight and a-half and nine in every shoe you have over there." He pointed the gun at the designer collection. He turned the gun back on them. "And if you try anything while your back there, I'll shoot her." He looked at Casey and sneered.

Lynn looked at Casey and hurried off to the stock room, returning with boxes of shoes and placing them on the counter. She went back to the stock room, while the other two men put the shoes in large cloth laundry bags. By the time they were done, the bags looked like Santa's gift sacks.

Lynn returned and placed another batch of boxes on the counter.

"That's it, they're all there."

The gunman pointed to one of his accomplices.

"Go back there with her. Make sure she's not trying to pull one over on us."

Lynn went into the stock room with one of the assailants on her heel. With Lynn gone longer than before, Casey began to worry. Lynn finally emerged and Casey felt her heart beat again.

"We got um all," the man said as he emerged from behind Lynn.

"Well, then that should do it. It was nice doing business with you," the gunman said before he turned to leave, when one of the other men who hadn't spoken before said, "wait a minute. What's in the bag?"

"A pair of shoes," Lynn said.

"Don't play smart with me. What size?" he continued.

"A seven and a-half, but it's not a designer shoe," Lynn highlighted.

"Hand it over."

Casey's hand trembled as he walked over and yanked the bag out of her hand. She grabbed the bag, "no, they're my shoes."

The gunman rushed over, and turned his gun to the side.

"Back away from the shoes, bitch!" Casey let go.

"You're one brave bitch, but brave bitches die," he said with the muzzle of the gun between

Casey's eyebrows. He eased the gun off her skin and walked over to the front door and they left with the bags over their shoulders.

Casey's heart felt like it was lodged in a crevice of her rib cage and it sent tremors through her entire body. Lynn waited until they disappeared into the dark alley before she picked up the phone to call the police. It didn't take long for them to arrive. Casey, numbed with fear, stood motionless in the store. *This wasn't how the adventure was supposed to end.*

CHAPTER EIGHT

The inside of the interrogation room reminded her of a restraint room minus the padded walls and straitjackets. A handsome mildly tanned officer with clean-cut light brown hair sat across from her with his gun holster tucked securely against the side of his ribcage. Casey managed to display a tense smile.

"Were there any distinct marks on any of the robbers?" Casey thought for a moment.

"Not really. They were completely covered. Not even the hairs on their heads were showing."
She lowered her head on the desk. The questions went on for over an hour. She looked at the clock. Her family had already eaten dinner, and she was starving.

"Actually, I noticed that one of the robber's goggles wasn't colored like the other two; his lens was clear and he had long eyelashes."

The officer jotted down what she said on the pad. He exhaled.

"Anything else?"

"No."

"If you think of anything else give us a call." He gave her his business card.

She walked through the lobby of the ninth precinct; officers took reports or walked perps to the holding cells. Casey looked up at the clock above the check in desk, 8:30 PM. If she wasn't home by 9 PM, she would have a lot of explaining to do. There was no way around it; she would have to tell them what happened. She took out her cell phone. She called the person who would freak out the least---her father.

"Hi Dad, I'm downtown. Can you pick me up?"

"Sure, your mom went to the grocery store with your brother."

"How soon can you be here?" Casey asked.

"It depends on where you are." Adam got in his truck.

"I'm at the ninth precinct."

Crickets were the only thing distinguishable in the silence that followed her sentence. Her father paused and his tone went into formal mode.

"I'll be there in about fifteen to twenty minutes. Are you okay?"

"I'm fine, dad."

"I'm on my way," Adam said before he ended the call.

She couldn't avoid a conversation with her father this time. He had every right to know why he was picking her up from the police station.

"Do I have to ask or are you going to tell me?"

"I was shopping at a boutique downtown, when three masked men robbed the store." Adam pulled over to the side of the road and turned off the engine.

"Did they hurt you?" He could deal with anything except someone hurting his children. Testing his metal in that way made him unpredictable.

"No, but one of them put a gun to my head and took the shoes I bought," Casey said and began to sob.

Adam hit the steering wheel, "If I catch those bastards, I'll beat the crap out of them."

Casey's eyebrows raised. She had never seen her dad this angry. He was normally as easy as apple pie on the taste buds. He hugged Casey.

"It will be okay. The police will catch them," Adam said.

A loud knock on the driver's side window, startled Adam. He turned, a bright light shown in his face temporarily blinding him. Then, the light was directed elsewhere and it gave him the opportunity to see a woman in front of his door and a flicker of what looked like a badge pinned to her chest. He put down the window, "Can I help you officer?"

"Are you stepping out of the car?" The officer asked.

"No, I parked to talk with my daughter."

"Is there a problem?"

"No, but we have been getting complains of people doing drugs on this strip in their cars," the officer said.

"Well I'm not one of them," Adam proclaimed. I'm having a conversation with my daughter."

"Carry on. We are here to keep you safe. If you see anything suspicious, give us a call."

"Absolutely," Adam said and put up his window and drove off.

"She scared the spit out of me," Casey said.

Adam got back on the road and they took the quickest route home. They pulled up in the driveway.

Kelly and Henry were already home by the time they got there. They entered the house and Adam kissed Kelly on the cheek. Kelly was packing away groceries and Henry was on the stool stocking canned goods in the pantry.

"Kelly I need to talk to you," Adam said. She stopped what she was doing.

"What's going on?"

"Come upstairs and let's talk," he insisted.

Kelly went up the staircase and Adam followed. Casey followed close behind and went to her room. She locked the door and flopped on the bed. Everything around her felt less secure. Her perfect world had been invaded by fear and she had to find a way to cope. Shortly after, she heard a knock on the door.

"Yes."

"It's Mom, can I come in?" Kelly asked.

"Yes."

"Are you okay?" Kelly stood next to her.

"Yes, under the circumstances."

"Your father told me what happened. If you need to talk, I'm here." Kelly wished she could do more to quell her fears.

"Thanks Mom," She hugged her mother.

"I'll give you some time to yourself." Kelly left the room.

CHAPTER NINE

Dreaming about what she would wear the next day was no longer the highlight of her dreams. Instead, the cold muzzle of a gun chilled her temple. Shortly after her shoes were ripped out of her hands, followed by the click of the trigger and *BANG*; she woke up. The only person who would understand her pain was Lynn. Casey had to see her.

Casey was fine until she got to Delancey Drive. She felt like the soles of her shoes were filled with cement when she arrived at Killer Shoes. She took a deep breath and entered the store. Lynn stood behind the counter arranging merchandise in the glass case. She looked up.

"How are you?"

"Terrible." Lynn's eyes filled with water. She came from behind the counter and walked to Casey.

"Every time the door opens, I get nervous. I can barely sleep and I feel like quitting this job so I can forget about what happened," said Lynn, her tears flowed freely down the sides of her cheeks.

Casey knew exactly what she was going through. They were survivors of a traumatic experience and it was unique to them. No one else could truly understand. They embraced.

"I'm having trouble sleeping too," Casey said.

"Do you think we will ever get over it?" Lynn asked.

"I don't know."

Casey spent an hour talking to Lynn between customers. She could work there if the robbery never happened. The employee discount would be an added benefit.

"So where are you going after you leave here?"

"I'm meeting my best friend Francesca at the Midland Ice-cream Parlor in front of our school."

"Sounds like fun," Lynn said.

Casey wrote down her phone number, "You can call me anytime."

"Thanks for coming by," Lynn said, as Casey left the store.

The modestly decorated building with glossy aluminum trim, blue awnings and a blue neon sign with the name Midland Ice Cream Parlor on the front was a popular hangout.

"Who ever invented the banana sundae deserves a kiss." Casey savored a spoonful of her sundae.

"Have you heard from the police?" Francesca asked.

"Nope, they'll call me when they have a lineup."

"What's new with you?" Casey asked. Francesca's yogurt ice cream looked like Mount Everest with toppings.

"Nothing, but I have a shadow."

"What are you talking about? We all have a shadow," Casey said.

"The boy from the mall, silly."

A young man walked into the parlor with a little girl. Casey looked in his direction, and then her eyes returned to the banana sundae.

"Isn't that the guy you were talking to at the Golden Nugget?"

Francesca looked over her shoulder.

"He's my shadow," Francesca sighed. Her interest in the pile of yogurt faded and the spoon fell to the wayside.

"I think he is stalking me."

"You're paranoid. Who is he?"

"Nu Gin. He goes to our school."

Casey looked at Nu, "He's hot." Francesca peaked over her shoulder, "I guess, but he's not my type."

"Do you even *have* a type?"

"Not really. I don't have time for boys right now."

Nu and his sister sat in the booth in front of them. When she was finished with her ice cream, she turned around and stared at Casey. After the first few seconds, Casey felt like an animal at the zoo. She still managed to smile and tried to focus on Francesca.

Her eyes strayed to the right of Francesca. The fleshy bulges above the young girl's eyelids made her eyes squinty and resembled the eye of a needle.

"I'm ready to go," Casey said.

The little girl strategically maneuvered her miniature doll on the top of Francesca's chair.

"Fine, I've lost my appetite." Francesca got up, her body brushed against the girl, and her toy fell into the depth of Francesca's seat.

"I'm sorry," Francesca picked up the toy and gave it to her.

The little girl took the toy, tucked it inside her shirt, and lowered her head. Nu turned around, "Hi Francesca." *If he says my name like that one more time, I'm going to scream.*

"Can you do me a favor?" Francesca said with flame to her voice. "Stop butchering my name."

Casey was surprised at her reaction. It wasn't like her to make something as simple as that bother her. People mispronounce names everyday all day. "Let's go Francesca, before you blow a gasket."

Francesca walked away and Casey lingered for a second, stopping at Nu's table. She whispered, "If you like her, don't give up." He smiled, and Casey walked away.

Maybe I stand a chance, but Francesca hates the way I say her name.

"Francesca, Francesca," Nu tried to pronounce her name. He looked at himself in the mirror in the boy's bathroom. *Girls are weird.*

"Francesca, Francesca."

"Shut up, I'm trying to concentrate," a boy shouted from the other end of the bathroom.

"Sorry!"

Nu had no idea why he was torturing himself in this way. He turned the faucet on and splashed cold water on his face. His black short hair with a modest

Mohawk was moussed to perfection and the sides were tapered, showing off his small ears.

Casey saw Nu leave the boy's bathroom while she was going to her second period class. He was as cute as Prada shoes, but Francesca was giving him a hard time. *Poor kid, I hope he figures it out.* She had her own problems to deal with. She would let them figure out the courtship games on their own.

It was a sunny day and many students gathered in the courtyard. Some sat on the picnic tables while others lay on blankets and read books under a shaded tree. Groups of boys played football. Casey and Francesca entered the courtyard and walked over to a bench at the other side of the lawn. Most students stayed at the other end because it was a long walk. Casey and Francesca maneuvered the maze of students that lounged on the manicured lawn.

"Are we still going to the mall this weekend?" Casey asked.

They heard a loud thump; Casey felt a quick breeze thrust across her back. Francesca's books fell to the ground. One of the players ran into Francesca, knocked her to the grass and he landed across her waist. She gasped for breath as his weight pinned her to the ground.

"Get up, you're hurting her!" Casey shouted. He took his time getting up, "I'm sorry I didn't see her."

"Maybe if you paid attention to the people around you instead of trying to catch balls, this wouldn't happen." Casey knelt at her side.

"I said I was sorry." He dusted off and walked away with the ball. The least he could do was help Francesca up or ask if she was okay.

She lay on the grass, hyperventilating.

Nu didn't see what happened, but he saw Francesca on the ground. He ran over to where they were.

"Is she okay?" he asked. Casey looked up, "I don't know."

"Can you walk?" Casey asked.

"I think so," she sat up and tried to stand, but a sharp pain shot up her leg.

"Ouch."

"She needs to go to the nurse. I can take her," Nu felt his medium frame could handle her weight.

"I think you should go see the nurse, Francesca," Casey said.

"Is it okay if I lift you and take you to the nurse, Francesca?"

He said my name right.

"Yes." He stooped down and lifted her. She wrapped her arms around his neck. Casey picked up Francesca's books and followed him to the nurse's office. All eyes were on them as they left the courtyard. Casey ran ahead to open the door for Nu.

Her head clung to his chest like Velcro.

"We're almost there," he said.

Casey knocked on the nurse's office door and entered.

"What do we have here?" the nurse said and put down the novel she was reading.

"She got tackled by one of the students who were playing football in the courtyard," Casey said.

"Put her over there on the bed by the window." The nurse pointed.

"Unbutton your shirt a bit," the nurse rested the stethoscope against her skin. Nu swallowed hard.

"I should go." He edged closer to the door.

"Thanks for bringing me to the nurses office," Francesca said.

"You're welcome." Nu slipped through the door.

Limping around with crutches wasn't exactly what Francesca envisioned in her future. A sprained ankle made navigating the halls treacherous. *Chivalry is dead*, with the exception of Nu; he was thoughtful and caring. She was such a snob to him in the ice cream parlor and he still came to her aid. His efforts upped his rating on the 'hot' meter.

The students at school reminded her of *Children of the Corn.* They anxiously waited to feast on the weak. The hierarchy of social status in their school didn't matter. When it all boiled down, it was a matter of 'survival of the fittest', 'work smarter not harder', and all that other bullshit. She felt sorry for the teachers; they were the ones who got the raw deal. They were stuck with babysitting other people's children without the option of using corporal punishment. Last year, she had seen a teacher in the fetal position in a corner crying after a run-in with a student who simply didn't give a fuck.

Whether they were a teacher or student, they were there to fulfill a need; either it was to get away from home, a means of financial support, an expected norm, or because there was nothing else to do, but they all had to make it through the day.

CHAPTER TEN

Mr. Reinhold missed his 11:30 AM appointment. Casey called his cell phone and left a message, but he did not respond. She had no choice but to cover for him, so he wouldn't lose clients.

"Mr. Reinhold was in a fender-bender just off the highway. He's waiting for a tow truck," Casey explained.

"That's unfortunate, I can reschedule," the client said. Lying wasn't required but it came with the territory.

By noon, Casey was ready to unwind. She lit a few scented candles. The air quickly filled with a raspberry vanilla aroma. A patterned tapping came through the hallway into the office. Casey looked at her appointment book. *Shit!*

"He has a 12:30 PM appointment."

The office door swung open. Her orange and blue Pierre Hardy heels stood out beneath the blue Dolce and Gabbana dress. Orli Rothman was always overdressed for the occasion, or perhaps casual wasn't a part of her vocabulary.

"Did I interrupt something?" Orli asked, as she entered the office.

"No. Come in."

"I'll have to reschedule your appointment. Mr. Reinhold won't be in today."

"That's unfortunate. I was hoping for an update on my case," Orli turned just in front of Casey's desk and sat in the leather chair. "I need the next available appointment," she said as Mr. Reinhold stumbled in with his shirt disheveled and covered in mud splotches.

Casey cleared her throat, "Did the tow truck pick up your vehicle from the accident site?"

"Uh, yeah right," he said and tucked in his shirt. Casey made a no gesture with her head. While Mrs. Rothman looked at him, "Oh my, are you okay?"

"I am fine. I was in an accident." Mr. Reinhold sure knew how to dispense deception when needed. "Just give me a few minutes to freshen up and I'll be with you shortly." He entered the bathroom.

Thomas looked at his reflection in the mirror. He looked like he was in a car accident but instead he was involved in a fight with a former client's husband. His endless pursuit of women-in-distress would be his downfall. He was tired of getting his ass kicked like a soccer ball. Mr. Reinhold understood the man's rage, but he wasn't sure how much more he could take before he got the police involved.

"I respect a man who comes to work after being in an accident. I would have gone home to the comfort of my bed," Orli said. Casey couldn't believe how gullible his clients were but she was an accomplice to their impression of him.

He emerged from the bathroom. "You can come in," Mr. Reinhold said before they disappeared into his office.

"The person in question has been under surveillance for two months and I haven't seen anything to indicate anything suspicious." He placed a file of photos in front of her and she looked through them.

"These are useless; they don't tell a story. What is done in the dark will come to light. Keep looking."

"I'd like to wrap up this investigation sooner than later. I'm paying you a handsome sum of money. So I expect results, Mr. Reinhold."

"I assure you, you'll get results," he said. Orli got up and left his office.

She walked past Casey, "Lose the candles; they're bad for your health."

Mrs. Rothman always had to have the last word. If she didn't, Casey was afraid she might spontaneously combust. The less one said around people like that the better. They'd gnaw at you mentally like a feral beast.

CHAPTER ELEVEN

Nu hung up his apron for the night and went for a stroll in the mall. He passed by Hot Topic. There was a crowd in there. He decided to have a look and backtracked. He stood outside the window and looked at the odd attractions inside.

"I didn't know you were into this kind of stuff," Francesca said as she stood next to him.

"Hi." He smiled, displaying deep-set dimples. His hypnotic smile was like accessible sunshine.

"I'm not. I wanted to see why so many people are in there."

Francesca held his hand, "let's find out."

Her skin was soft as silk and it sent chills up his arm. Nu felt like he had died and gone to heaven. They went inside and looked around at the accessories. Emo music pumped from the large speakers braced to the walls. A disco ball sent glistening lights throughout the store and reflected on the customers. The selections got riskier the further they went in the store. Grunge t-shirts hung off cage-like racks inscribed with risqué phrases, '*Ass, I am a fan, I'm Addicted to Weed and Speed, and I Put The STD In Stud But All I Need Is U.*' They went to the back, where a rack of G-strings, feathered boas, and bustier bras lined the walls. Nu was embarrassed, and Francesca felt practically naked. He had no idea they sold that kind of stuff in the mall.

"I think I've seen enough." His face stiffened.

"Me too." Once they passed the exit, Francesca burst out laughing. "I think we deserve ice cream."

Nu blushed, "I agree."

They strolled over to Coldstone Creamery, ordered up a hearty size of ice cream, and sat in a secluded corner of the store.

"How's your ankle?"

"It's better." Francesca extended her legs. Nu saw her manicured toes and admired her bronze wedge sandal.

She played with her ice cream for a moment, "I'm sorry for being mean to you."

"It's okay; I pronounced your name wrong."

"Yes but it's not a good excuse to be a snob. I appreciate what you did for me in the courtyard the other day."

She could do worse. Francesca heard of many horror stories about young men who mistreated girls they liked or dated. Nu was different, as easy as a summer breeze and calm under pressure.

"It was my pleasure. I'm sorry it had to happen under those circumstances." He spun a quarter on the table. George Washington's face displayed when it landed.

Henry's face was the first thing Casey saw when she walked into the living room. He slouched in the beanbag chair that he brought downstairs from his room.

"Hi, Henry." She sat in the sofa behind him. "What are you watching?"

"Madagascar."

"Oh, I love that movie. Do you mind if I watch it with you?"

"Sure, I don't mind."

Henry's pug wobbled in a few minutes later. He circled the living room like a dog at the Westminster Dog Show. At the end of his round, Randy farted and sat next to Henry. *Like boy like dog.* His fart spread like a mushroom cloud of a bomb.

Casey pinched her nose, "My god, what are you feeding him?"

"Lots of stuff. He eats popcorn, chips, ice cream, cake…"

"I get the picture. No wonder he's so gassy." She released her nose. The scent faded, but remnants remained. The room smelled like a ripe garbage truck was parked nearby.

Randy rolled unto his back. Henry tickled his belly and Randy giggled like a hyena.

Casey was tired of watching Madagascar. She went upstairs, and saw rose petals lining the hall. The petals led to her parent's room and soft music lingered in the hallway. Casey entered her room and jumped on her bed. At least her parents were happy and in love. She would never see her mom at Mr. Reinhold's detective agency. Casey was glad tomorrow was Friday.

While other students were bombarded with information, an hour-and-a-half after waking up, Casey relaxed in study hall, listened to music on the down low or read a book. She had given up her study hall time to tutor Francesca. If she needed help, there was no doubt in her mind that Francesca would have her back.

"I swear that turd-in-a-skirt is as annoying as the YouTube song, *Friday*," Casey said. It was times like these she wished she had super powers. Casey would evaporate Clarissa's trifling ass into dust, but that's not all; she would give her ashes to Keith Richards so he could smoke them.

"She's not important, besides I need you to focus on helping me study for my algebra test." Francesca was nose deep in study sheets and a textbook thicker than the Bible.

"There are more complex subjects than Algebra. When you get to college, Algebra will be easy compared to Calculus and Trigonometry."

"Trigonometry sounds like an incurable disease." She got a good laugh out of Casey.

"I'll keep that in mind but I'm confused. The textbook showed long-winded examples with ten steps before you got to the answer. Mr. Robins showed us various ways instead of showing the simplest way."

"I understand what you're saying but the simplest way doesn't show the stuff that goes on in between," Casey explained.

Francesca's face soured, "I hate math!"

"You'll pass. Relax," Casey said. "I just wish she would stop going out of her way to annoy me."

"I have never done anything to her. I don't know what her problem is." Casey babbled on.

"I think I know. In the sixth grade, Kendrick Reynolds wrote you a note, and tossed it in your direction but Clarissa intercepted it. She read the note, crushed it in a ball and hurled it at you," Francesca recalled.

"I remember; the note read, 'if you like me, check yes or no.'" Casey laughed.

"It's a long time to hold a grudge. They say holding grudges cause's wrinkles. It's not your fault he didn't like her," Francesca said.

"Anyway, I have to go to my second period class. Maybe we can meet at the ice cream parlor after school?"

"Actually, I'm meeting Nu there after school." Casey's eyebrows rose. She smiled, "give me a call later." She was glad Francesca warmed up to him. She thought they made a cute couple.

CHAPTER TWELVE

"Casey, Detective Ramos left a message for you on the answering machine," Kelly said.

"Thanks mom." She listened to the message.

"Your dad said he'll take you when he gets home." Later in the afternoon, Adam called.

He was working on a construction project that was close to the deadline, so he asked his wife to take Casey to the police station.

When they arrived at the ninth precinct, it was hectic inside. Casey looked at her mother from the corner of her eye. The police station was a zoo of sorts, filled with hookers, gangsters, and the most elusive...white-collar criminals in a room. It was no wonder that cops were naturally suspicious of everyone. They have seen the worst in the best of us and it came with the territory. Detective Ramos emerged from a back office.

"Come with me. We have some perps I'd like you to see." She followed him to a secluded area and entered a soundproofed room with a large window. Six men walked into the well-lit room with height markers and stood against the wall. Her heart raced.

"Do you see anyone that fits the description of the robbers?" he asked.

"I don't know," Casey stammered.

"They can't see you. If there's anyone that looks familiar, let me know."

"No."

"Are you sure?"

"Yes." Casey reiterated.

The men were moved to a holding area. Casey and the detective left the room a few minutes later.

"We'll call you if we come up with new suspects," Detective Ramos said. She walked out to the front waiting area.

"How did it go?" Kelly asked. She walked to Casey.

"Life would be grand if the police found the ones responsible for the robbery," Casey said.

"Yes but it's easy for you to say and hard for the police to do," Kelly said.

"Let's go somewhere for a few hours. I know I haven't had much time for you and Henry lately. Work has been crazy."

Casey's eyes traveled in every direction. "I get it mom, but family comes first."

"Absolutely, but in order to take care of our family your father and I have to work."

"Casey bowed her head. "I know. So, where are we going?"

"Bowling!" I've always wanted to but never got around to it."

"Okay, let's go," Casey said.

The bowling alley smelled like aged leather, and the floor gave off a healthy glow of their reflection. It was early in the evening and there were only a few people inside. They stretched to prime their bodies for the task.

"Let it rip," Casey sent the ball rolling down the lane. It rolled into the gutter and left all the pins standing.

"Bummer!"

"My turn." Kelly stooped and swayed the ball between her legs. "Buckaroo Bonsai!" Kelly tossed the ball with both hands. Casey laughed.

"Mom, I don't know much about bowling, but that's not the way to throw the ball." The ball veered off to the left and knocked two pins down.

"Yeah!" Kelly pranced up and down. They played for another hour, and by then they both had something to brag about.

"That's the most fun I've had in a while. Thanks. I really needed that," Casey said.

Her Mom hugged her. "Anytime."

"Let's get home before your father puts an APB out on us."

CHAPTER THIRTEEN

Casey went to Killer Shoes to browse the new arrivals. Though they had a wide selection for her occasion, she didn't get the feeling she felt before. When she found her perfect shoes, her toes tingled. Casey saw a pair of shoes that reminded her of the shoes that had been stolen from her. Her heart ached when she relived having them yanked out of her hand. In that instant, she remembered something, but lost her chain of thought when Francesca entered the store.

"You were right. Killer Shoes is fabulous with a capital *F*." Francesca's eyes traveled around the room. "I'm not as picky as you are with shoes. I know I'll find a pair for the prom here."

"I knew you would like it. It's like Willy Wonka's Chocolate Factory. Once you've walked inside, you don't want to leave empty-handed. You can never have enough pairs of shoes."

Francesca was all over the place; she couldn't make up her mind.

"Why don't you look at what you can afford?" Francesca raised one brow and gave Casey a knowing look.

"I doubt that's what you did when you were here," Francesca said. Casey smirked and avoided eye contact.

"Shame on you," Francesca said with a smirk, "Don't deprive me of the pleasure of trying on some bliss in a shoe."

Casey bobbled her head, "Okay, I tried on all of the designer shoes I liked in my size before moving on to the selections I could afford."

"Guess what?" Francesca was excited.

"I give up. What is it?" Casey said immediately.

"I passed my Algebra test."

"Sweet." Casey high-fived Francesca, "You passed the test."

"Yup! And Nu asked me to the prom."

"That's great. I'm so happy for you."

Francesca lined up three pairs of shoes. "Thanks. I'm down to these. Which ones do you like the most?"

"They're all beautiful, but I like the ones in the middle. You're going to light up the dance floor with those shoes."

"I plan to. The search is over. Time to pay up and move on," Francesca said.

"Nice choice." Lynn went behind the counter. "We also have the matching clutch." Lynn walked to the end of the glass counter, opened the case and placed the clutch on the counter.

"I'll take them both."

"Lynn, have you heard anything from Detective Ramos?"

"Yes, I went down to the station for a line-up but it was a waste of time. The robbers weren't there." Casey hadn't heard from the police since her line-up. She hated the thought of the robbers getting away with their criminal activities. It was an injustice to say the least.

"Well, we'll be on our way. See you next time," Casey said, and left the store.

"Take care," Lynn said as she emerged from behind the counter to organize the shoe racks.

The sky was slightly overcast and the low humidity made it a perfect day for a stroll.

They walked to the waterfront and sat on a bench that lined the boardwalk. Casey gazed quietly at the river. The waves were a treadmill of constant motion and it calmed her. A Jet Ski pranced in the water, and another followed close behind. The Jet Ski's swerved and chased one another like birds and prey.

"I love it here," Casey said.

"I am looking forward to our sleepover this weekend. It's been awhile," Francesca said.

Casey smiled when she recalled past sleepovers.

"What's the theme this time?"

"The Seventies!" Francesca said. A thought cloud surfaced and Francesca relived some of their past silly antics.

"I'm going to have to raid the attic, and go through my mom's old stuff," Casey said.

"We're going to have a blast."

Francesca and Casey walked past vending carts that sold exotic delicacies under large wooden market umbrellas. The aroma of the food summoned customers. They decided to try the food and waited in line at the Korean BBQ vending cart. Casey ordered the BBQ chicken on a stick and Francesca got spicy Kimchi.

Casey glared at her, and looked at the bowl of Kimchi. "What is it?"

Francesca smiled. "Pickled cabbage."

"Gross." Casey cringed. They sat on a bench and gazed at the water.

Once the sun curtsied, the vintage streetlights that dotted the boardwalk in front of the stores lit up. The lights created a soft reflection on the surface of the river. Indistinguishable chatter filled the air, and wine poured freely into eager glasses alongside dinner under the moonlight. Street vendors closed down and pushed their carts away. The vendors passed Casey and Francesca and Casey on their way out of the waterfront.

"It's getting late. We should go," Casey said and got up.

Francesca looked at her watch and stood up. "Yes it is. Let's go," and they left the waterfront.

CHAPTER FOURTEEN

Randy wobbled into her room with a bowtie around his neck.

"The party mascot is here." Casey chuckled. Her attention returned to the computer.

"Henry, did you give Randy ice cream yesterday or today?" Casey asked in an elevated tone.

"No," Henry said as he walked to her room.

"Good. The last thing we need is Randy going on a gas fest. It would be the ultimate party pooper."

Henry walked in wearing a busy print shirt with a popped collar and tight high-water jeans. "What do you think?" He turned around.

"Henry, are your ankles are saying something?" Casey laughed.

"What?" He looked confused.

"Cover me!" Francesca and Casey had a good laugh at his expense.

They looked online at the 70's fashions and went through pages of fashions where nothing matched, at least not on purpose.

Casey was stuck on one picture of a handsome young man with muscular legs in tight pants; his legs had no room to breathe.

The girls were no better; their pants were high in the crotch area.

"Back then, girls liked guys who wore tight pants," Casey laughed. They were eager to see what they'd look like when they were dressed.

Casey fared well in a peach mini dress, a scarf was tied around the crown of her head and platform boots adorned her feet. Francesca's long tresses were traded in for a tailored afro wig. She tucked an afro pick with a fist at the end in the back of the afro. She accentuated the look with bell-bottoms, hoop earrings, and a crop shirt tied in front.

The usual objects on the top of her dresser were replaced with trays of snacks, beverages and a two-tier cake. Even Randy had his own plate, a paper plate. She had no problem sharing food with his pet, but hell would serve cool drinks before she'd eat out of a plate Randy slobbered on.

The more sugar they ingested, the louder they became. To add to the noise factor, Casey put on the stereo her parents loaned her for the sleepover. They were nice enough to sweeten the pot with their 70's music collection. Bohemian Rhapsody, Hotel California, and Summer Breeze bellowed from the speakers.

The night was going well. As things calmed down, they watched *Three's Company*, *Bosom Buddies* and *Alfred Hitchcock*. By 2:20 AM, they were fast asleep on the floor or on the bed, and Randy fell asleep with his face in a plate of cake and chips.

Henry's eyes opened, and it took every ounce of his energy to sit up. A growling sound came from the walls of his stomach and his body went through short spurts of temperature changes. He swallowed hard to fight the unsettled feeling rising in his throat. Foul bile spilled to the floor, followed by a hacking cough. The souvenirs of a night before painted a Picasso with all-you-can-eat junk food on the floor.

Their noses sniffed unconsciously in their sleep as the sourness of Henry's vomit settled. Casey woke first and Francesca woke a few minutes after she felt movement on the bed.

"Come on Henry, you could have tried to make it to the bathroom," Casey said. She was pissed, but before she had a chance to shout, she added to Henry's collage with a shade of her own vomit.

Francesca was dumbfounded, "I'm going to the bathroom." She hurried out of the room and ran down the hall. Francesca made it as far as the bathroom door before she vomited on the tiles.

"Shit! Your mom's going to kill me."

Casey followed her.

"Nah, we've done this before, in the sixth grade."

Francesca wiped drool from the corner of her mouth. "Yes, I remember." She managed to smile even though her stomach felt like she'd been on a roller coaster ride.

"Let's clean up the mess we've made before we give my parents something to complain about. My mom can be a stickler when it comes to keeping the house in order. You know what they say, 'When mom's happy, everyone's happy!'"

The brim of their stomachs almost overflowed. They came downstairs to a breakfast buffet Casey's mom had prepared.

"I think I'm going to be sick again," Casey said. "I'll just have some tea. I can't eat anything else."

Kelly glanced in their direction, "Where's Henry?"

"He's in the bathroom."

"Do you want anything to eat Francesca?"

"No thank you, I have a stomach ache."

Francesca and Casey went into the living room to watch television. Casey flipped through the channels and stopped on the morning news.

"This is Abbey Walsh reporting from the Woodberry Mall. Last night an hour before closing time, four masked men robbed Claire's Boutique at gunpoint. Two employees were hurt during the robbery. A male employee was assaulted with a gun and a female employee was sexually assaulted.

The robbers have expensive taste. All of the items taken were designer shoes. When more information becomes available, we'll keep you updated. Abbey Walsh, Channel 7 News."

Casey looked at Francesca, "something has to be done about this."

"Casey," Kelly called from the dining room.

"Yes, mom," Casey got up and went into dining room.

"I need you to look after your brother this evening. Your dad and I have plans."

"Sure, no problem."

That's a first, Casey always complained about watching Henry. "Are you and your brother getting along?"

"Yes, we've come to an understanding. If he behaves, we get along and do cool stuff together, or we can make each other's life miserable."

"Good for you. I'm glad you too are getting along."

Francesca went home once her stomach settled. Henry and Casey spent the better part of the afternoon trying to outrun one another to the bathroom. Randy was in the hall on his back, looking like a dog that had far too many drinks. They walked around him and went on their way, but Randy took his liberty a bit further. He passed gas and Adam banned him from the house for the day. Randy sure knew how to have a good time and now he was paying for it. The day progressed and her stomach settled but she was exhausted. The weight of her eyelids made it hard to keep her eyes open as she lay on the couch. Casey saw a flicker of the shoe on her mother's feet and opened her eyes.

Kelly looked stunning. A gray cap-sleeve dress hugged her petite frame and gray appliqué *Sadi* peep-toe pumps adorned her feet.

"What's the occasion mom?"

"A celebration of love. Isn't that enough?"

Casey shrugged her shoulders, "I don't know."

"Someday you'll understand."

Her father emerged in a suit and Kelly just about melted. "I'll excuse myself," Casey said. She got the feeling they would like some privacy. Kelly turned to the mirror to put on her earrings. Adam walked up behind her.

"You look lovely." He held her hair aside, she inserted an earring, and he kissed her on the neck.

"Adam," she closed her eyes briefly, "Don't get me started. We have plans," Kelly said and her breath quickened. Adam turned her around, cupped the sides of her chin and pressed his lips against hers. Their lips danced the tango, and for a moment, they forgot about their plans.

The Sullivan's returned home from their outing and parked in the driveway.

"That was fun." Kelly kissed Adam before they left the car and entered through the kitchen door.

"Oh come on," Kelly said in agitation as they entered the living room. Henry and Casey were asleep on the sofa. DVD cases, popcorn, and empty soda cans littered the living room floor.

"Casey!" Adam shouted.

She jerked to attention. "Did you have the fellows over from the Hangover movie?" Adam asked. Casey looked confused. She was neither awake nor asleep.

She looked around the room. "Sorry, I was going to clean up before you got home but I fell asleep." She nudged Henry.

He woke up and looked around the room, "oh-oh."

"Come on Henry let's get the room in order."

"There's no need to swallow your heart, but don't let it happen again. Hide the evidence for god's sake." Adam smiled when he walked away.

CHAPTER FIFTEEN

Casey had a long night; getting up to go to school was the last thing she wanted to do but she had no say in the matter. The day seemed longer due to minimal sleep she got the night before. Her mind kept wondering off to distant places. Casey sat at her desk; her pencil steadily tapped the Formica, when she felt a thud at the back of her shoes. She bit her lip, *I swear if this—*.

"Casey, read the first two paragraphs in the text please," Mrs. Phillips instructed. Casey tried not to stumble on any words. When she was done, Mrs. Phillips moved on to the next victim. Clarissa was lucky, Casey wasn't in the mood.

What she heard on the news troubled her. Casey shook her head. The robbers struck again, but this time someone was hurt. Casey didn't think so at the time, but they were lucky to escape the ordeal unharmed.

Francesca's third period teacher dismissed them, so she went to study hall to pass time until her next class. Sissy was there, perched at a corner table.

"Hi." Francesca sat in front of Sissy. She stopped doodling.

"Hi, how are you?" Sissy closed her book.

"I'm good."

"Are you going to the prom?"

"Yes," Francesca beamed with excitement. Sissy had never seen Francesca this happy.

"So it's like that. Are you going with someone special?" Sissy asked.

"Yes."

"I don't have a date, but I'm going anyway. I got a good deal on a designer shoe," Sissy said.

"I wish you had told me before I bought mine."

"That's okay. I can hook you up next time. Let me know and I'll give my contact a call."

Francesca shrugged her shoulders, "okay."
It was hard to take Sissy seriously. She has a cute face, but her red curly hair diverted the onlooker's attention. Sissy's hair looked like a prehistoric bird's nest. Francesca swore any minute a pterodactyl would land on her head.

"My class will start soon, See you later."

On her way to class, Francesca bumped into Casey.

"Are we going to hang out after school?"

"No, I have to work today, but I'll call you later." Casey hurried off to her next class.

CHAPTER SIXTEEN

When Casey arrived at the office, Mr. Reinhold was already there and someone was in his office. It didn't take long for her to figure out it was Orli Rothman. She cringed. Mr. Reinhold kept Mrs. Rothman busy while Casey dug up information about her online.

She was right; Orli was financially fit. She was involved with children's charities and sponsored a holiday gift drive for wards of the state. Orli was a snob, but it appeared she had a good heart. Mr. Reinhold came out of his office, "I thought I heard you come in."

"Did you need anything?" Casey asked.

"No, but I'd like you to hold my calls until I'm finished with the client." He went back into his office and closed the door.

Casey got up, tipped the blinds upward to lessen the glare of the sun and returned to her desk. She scrolled through pages of information. Mr. Reinhold's office door opened and the door hinges squeaked. Orli stepped out, "You should oil the joints," she said.

Casey rolled her eyes. *I think she'd shrivel up and die if she couldn't make annoying comments.*

Mrs. Rothman's clothing was a blank canvas, but she still managed to make an indelible impression. She was draped in a white Diane Von Furstenberg dress, which was a cross between a classic button-down shirt and a pleated skirt, accessorized in a vintage link bracelet with a white peep toe Christian Louboutin heels. Mrs. Rothman looked as though she had stepped off a Vogue cover. *Damn! I would like to walk a mile in her shoes.*

"Goodbye, for now." She walked daintily out the door.

Orli left, but it didn't deter Casey's curiosity.

A burly man opened the office door. When it swung open, the knob made a loud thud when it connected with the wall. He walked swiftly inside Mr. Reinhold's office.

"Hey, wait!" Casey shouted, but it was too late; he had already entered and closed the door behind him. Loud noises erupted soon after and it sounded like a martial arts special effects crew had set up shop in there. She moved closer to the door and knocked, "Is everything okay? Would you like me to call the police?" Her hands trembled as she held the doorknob. The disturbance paused.

"No," he managed to blurt out before the noises returned.

Oh well, she respected his wishes. What he did with his life was none of her business.

Ten minutes later, the man emerged, straightened his jacket, gave Casey a 'Death to America' stare and left the office. Mr. Reinhold staggered out moments later and collapsed on the floor. She shook him, but he didn't respond.

"I'm sorry Mr. Reinhold but I have to call an ambulance."

The EMT asked so many questions but she had no answers. She was mad enough to blow a gasket. If he didn't want the police involved, then that also applied to the EMT's. She was young, but she knew police and medical professionals were blood brothers.

"I don't know what happened, but he needs medical attention," Casey said. The EMT looked at her and then shifted his attention to Mr. Reinhold. They poked around his body, and took note of his injuries. When the EMT touched a spot on Thomas's chest, he woke up and thrust forward in pain.

"What the hell…didn't I say not to call anyone?" he shouted. His eyes were bloodshot and the side of his lip was swollen.

"Yes, but you collapsed."

He exhaled and laid back on the gurney, "I'm sorry, I shouldn't have shouted."

He turned his attention to the EMT, "I am refusing medical attention at this time. I'll go to my private physician." The EMT packed up his gear, Mr. Reinhold got off the gurney and they left the office.

"This is none of my business, but you've made it my business when your bully came in here and scared the snot out of me. What's going on Mr. Reinhold?" The temperature of her blood went up a notch. "Tell me or today will be my last day!"

He slumped down against the wall. He looked defeated.

"I owe him five-hundred-thousand dollars."

Casey's jaw lowered, "that's a lot of money."

"Why do you owe him five-hundred-thousand dollars?"

"I don't want to bore you with the details."

"Bore me!" Casey joined him on the floor. "I sold him, The Plane Has Landed..."

"What?"

"It's the name of a retired prized horse. Owners come up with catchy phrases so that when their horse wins, the announcer will say something cool like, *The Plane Has Landed* won the race."

"So what's the problem?" Casey asked.

"He was my father's horse. When my father died, I inherited him. I sold Buddy a decoy and sold *The Plane Has Landed* to someone else for a million dollars."

Casey's eyes widened.

"He found out after someone tipped him off. Hence, he tuned me up a couple of times for his money."

"Why don't you pay him if you got a cool million for the horse?"

He shrugged his shoulders, "I blew the money betting on a few horses."

And they say teenagers do dumb stuff, but some adults are no better.

"What are you going to do?" she asked.

"I don't know just yet, but I'll figure it out." Although Mr. Reinhold's ordeal was an attention grabber, she could deal with his issues later, if he was still alive.

After the craziness that occurred at work yesterday, Casey needed to unwind. She walked through the mall aimlessly before she sat down in a massage chair. Francesca sat in the chair next to her and inserted a dollar in the money slot. A dollar provided three minutes of lower back manipulation. For now, they were content. They watched others stroll the mall. Casey looked up at the sunroof; light shone in on the escalators and highlighted the shoppers as they moved from level to level.

"I should start looking for a replacement pair of shoes," Casey said. *I can't mope over a stolen pair forever.*

"I don't know why you waited so long; it will be hard to find a nice pair this close to the dance."

"Sissy can probably hook you up with something nice from an acquaintance of hers," Francesca said.

Casey gave Francesca a weird glance, "do you mean Nuttier than squirrel turd Sissy?"

"Yup, that's the one."

"Nope. That's okay."

CHAPTER SEVENTEEN

She hated those moments when all she heard was the tick-tock from the clock on the wall. Those dull moments made the workday go by slowly. Casey sat at her desk; her eyes traveled the wood paneled walls. She tried to look busy. Her eyes traveled the room before they landed on the face of her watch. Mr. Reinhold was late for his appointment with Mrs. Rothman. Orli decided to wait. Occasionally, Orli glanced at her watch, then at her, and it was Casey's cue to smile.

Casey hoped Mr. Reinhold got there before Orli started to comment on everything under the sun. Mrs. Rothman crossed her legs and Casey got a view of her Brian Atwood pale-pink suede platform pumps with a crystal-coated heel.

"Do you like working here?"

"Yes. It has its moments."

"Are you a student?" Orli continued her questioning.

"Yes. I'm a junior in high school."

Orli smiled. "You're almost done."

"Do you have any children?" Casey asked.

"Yes." Orli's eyes perked. "But I wouldn't put myself through the horrors of childbirth. I adopted my children."

Just then, Mr. Reinhold walked into the office. Usually she was glad to see him, but she wished he had stayed away longer.

"Forgive me Mrs. Rothman; I was on a surveillance assignment."

"It's okay, your receptionist kept me entertained."

"I think I have what you're looking for. Have a seat in my office." He said exactly what she wanted to hear. Mr. Reinhold walked over to the file cabinet and retrieved a file. He placed the folder in front of Orli. She opened the file and looked at its contents.

"I have operatives working to infiltrate the group, but they're very selective." Mr. Reinhold turned a pen between his thumb and index fingers, easing back in his chair.

CHAPTER EIGHTEEN

She sat atop the closed lid of the toilet in silence. The sound of running water echoed in the hollow bathroom as Casey washed her hands. It was a shame that she had to eavesdrop from the bathroom to get the information she desired. Mrs. Rothman's case was the big Kahuna out of all of the other cases she had dealt with since she started working there. Something was going on in Paradise Falls, Maine and Orli was determined to find out what it was.

Why would Orli Rothman, a wealthy woman, care about infiltrating an organization? The less things made sense, the more Casey felt the urge to uncover the truth. She left the bathroom, just as Mr. Reinhold emerged from his office.

"Put this away please." He gave Casey a file and it slipped from her hands. Sheets of paper and photos spilled on the floor. There wasn't enough time to read, but pictures are worth a million words.

To her surprise, when Casey got home from work, her parents had plans to take the family out to Bradley's, a popular five star restaurant downtown. She was content with her mother's cooking but she'd be a fool to pass up a place like Bradley's where they cooked the food practically on your lap. She looked at her brother. When Henry wore a tie, he looked adorable.

Kelly and Adam armed themselves with a glass of champagne, while Henry and Casey settled for cider. Casey waited patiently and observed the full restaurant with low elegant lighting. Jazz and classical undertones streamed from the vintage jukebox. Their chef dressed in white, with a matching toque hat, skillfully tossed an array of vegetables. The aroma of soy sauce, portabella mushrooms, red onions and basil spread across the table. Henry sneezed, sending a kaleidoscope of germs into the pit of his bent arm.

"Excuse me." Henry wiped the remnants of saliva off his arm with a napkin.

"You're excused!" Casey said.

"Thanks for bringing us to this nice restaurant," Casey paused for a moment, "but why are we here?"

"Well," Kelly pursed her lips, "I have an announcement." A soft squeal followed.

Oh boy, please don't let it be a baby! One sibling is enough.

"The project I've been working on was so successful that I was promoted to the position of executive marketing director," Kelly said in a bubbly tone.

"Congratulations mom, you deserve it," Casey said.

Henry smiled displaying a half-grown front tooth.

"Good girl," Henry said and they laughed.

"I'm proud of you honey." Adam kissed Kelly's hand.

"I'd like to make a toast." Adam raised his glass. "To new beginnings." Their glasses met in tribute of Kelly's accomplishment.

The chef shared out two steamy stir-fry beef with vegetables for Casey and Henry.

The food was exquisite; the beef was soft and succulent. It was nothing like the chewing gum version Kelly prepared at home. Kelly and Adam's surf and turf looked like the perfect marriage of mammoth lobster tails and a prime moon of beef.

Kelly savored the taste. "I've heard about this place for a while and they were right; the food is delicious." Kelly wiped the corners of her mouth. Henry separated the strips of beef from the sautéed vegetables.

"Eat your vegetables," Adam said and Henry pouted. "You always eat your vegetables at home. What's wrong?"

"Actually Dad, Randy always…"

Henry kicked Casey in the shin.

"Ouch!" Casey got up, "I have to use the restroom. May I be excused?"

"Sure," Kelly said.

Casey left the table and traveled down the pathway to the bathroom. She opened the door to see marble countertops with 24-karat gold fixtures, cathedral style mirrors above the sinks, and large paintings gracing the walls. It was arguably one of the most elegant bathrooms in Paradise Falls. She took out her cell phone and sent Francesca a text message. *Meet me at the ice cream parlor after school. It's important.*

One of the bathroom stall doors opened, a squeaking sound followed. Casey glanced over her shoulder to see Orli Rothman walking over to the sink and turning on the faucet.

"They should put oil on that," Casey said. Orli looked at her from the corner of her eyes as she washed her hands.

"Yes, they should."

Casey's mind went into overdrive and parked on Dare Devil Hill. She cleared her throat; "Mr. Reinhold's undercover operative has successfully infiltrated the organization."

"Really?" Orli said. Casey had her attention. She had to follow up with something convincing or else Orli would walk away. *Think! Think!*

"There appears to be an illegal operation going on."

Orli's facial expression tensed, "I've noticed he's extremely careful and when someone is that careful they're hiding something."

Orli didn't know that Casey was as clueless to the situation as she was.

"Yes, he's clever and knows how to cover his tracks," Casey said.

"I've learned about a place he frequents." Orli wrote on a pad she took out of her purse. "This is the address. Give it to Mr. Reinhold."

"I will." Orli left the bathroom and Casey simmered in self-admiration. The new information gathered by rapid-fire lying could be useful.

CHAPTER NINETEEN

Casey entered the address in the internet search, 3714 Bullworth Lane. It came up as the address for an entertainment spot called Dave & Buster's. She'd heard of the place from kids at school, but it was on the other side of town. Casey had no desire to go to that part of town, but if she wanted to find out anything about Mrs. Rothmans case, she had to go whether she liked it or not.

After a convincing round of begging, Adam agreed to take Casey, Francesca and Henry to Dave & Buster's. They arrived at the unimpressive mall location with lack luster signage. Adam looked around.

"There are a few empty spots in the mall." He got out of the truck and hesitated for a while. Weeds grew from cracks in the parking lot.

"Come on Dad, let's go." Henry tugged at Adam's jeans.

Francesca and Casey walked ahead to the entrance.

"So, do you have any new information on the case?" Francesca asked in a hushed tone.

"Kind of. I'll tell you about it later."

The inside of Dave & Buster's was bigger than she expected. They walked through the reserved party area, and arrived at the general eating area with booth style seating.

"Welcome to D&B, how many in your party?" the waiter asked.

"Four."

"We have a table available across from the bar. Is that okay?"

"That's fine," Adam said.

"Follow me, please." The waiter led them to their table.

Lights blinked above a large bar in the center of the dining room. Behind the dining room was an arcade. The constant chatter of amused adults and happy children confirmed that the D & B was the place to be on the weekend.

"I like the setup. It's really nice," Adam said.

"Dad! Can I have some change to play video games? Please dad."

"Okay, but after you eat so one of them can keep an eye on you. You can get lost in a place like this." The waiter approached their table.

"Are you ready to place your order?" the waiter asked. "I'd like a Coors light and the Kicking Spitting Chicken with fries. My son would like the cheeseburger special and a sprite."

The waiter smirked. "It has seven different peppers in the marinade."

"I can handle it." Adam perked his chest.

"We'll have two Eiffel burgers. Hold the mayo, onions and pickles please. One sweet tea and a sprite," Casey said.

"Would you like your drinks now or just before the food arrives?"

"When the food is ready, but we'll have water for now," Adam said.

Fifteen minutes later, the waiter returned with their drinks and the food. The Eiffel burgers were hard to devour. It took both hands to handle the beast of a sandwich. The Kicking Spitting Chicken was delicious but it was Arizona-summer hot. Adam guzzled down two glasses of water but the heat continued to rise in his throat. Henry happily ate his cheeseburger and fries. Half way through her sandwich, Casey felt a burning sensation in her chest. She pushed her plate forward.

"That's all I can take."

Francesca managed to eat three-quarters of her sandwich before she surrendered. They looked at Adam's face that was red from the heat of the peppers.

"Eating something super-sweet might help dad."

Adam signaled the waiter. A telling smirk spread across the waiters face.

"I need another glass of water and a banana foster."

"Your mother wiggled her way out of bringing you all here, but I think she would've liked it."

When Henry finished eating, they went to the arcade with the other patrons. Henry settled on Tekken 3, while Casey and Francesca played a racing game. It didn't take long for them to get tired of playing. It was hard to stay on the road, unless you were a pro on the home version.

"Let's switch with Henry," Francesca nudged him.

"Okay!" He hopped into the driver seat and drove like a madman.

Francesca went over to the Tekken game but a man beat her to the coin slot.

"Shit!" Francesca walked over to Casey's side and watched them race.

"Weren't you supposed to swap with Henry?" Casey asked.

"Yeah, but Mr. 'Fast and Furious' over there," she pointed, "beat me to it." Casey looked over at the Tekken game. She zoomed in on his crude face, wild eyebrows, and the fresh stubble around his jaw line.

He looked in their direction and smiled. Francesca rolled her eyes at him. Henry made Casey and Francesca look like chumps. He managed to finish the race in second place. Casey ran off the road and called it quits.

She got up and whispered in Francesca's ear, "Let's try the game behind us."

They moved on to an easier game. The only thing this game required the user to do was shoot the target. Francesca went first. It gave Casey time to observe the man on the Tekken game.

Two men came over to him and greeted him with a three-stage hand gesture. They talked, but it was so noisy she couldn't hear a word. They walked away a few minutes later and walked past Casey. One of them made eye contact.

"I'll be right back." Casey followed them. In the walkway in front of the reserved area, one of them stopped, took out his cell phone and made a call. Casey increased her pace.

"Yeah. We will meet at the usual spot and go over the specifics."

Casey walked by and heard the bones of the conversation. They turned around and went back into the common eating area.

Francesca leveled up fast in the shooting game. The more points she made, the less she paid attention to her surroundings. Casey walked up next to her. She didn't realize Casey was back until she looked to her right.

"Do you want to play?" Francesca shouted over the noise.

"Yes." They traded places. Francesca went back to the racing game. Henry was still going strong, but he was bored. There were so many games to choose from that being weary wouldn't last very long.

A couple walked away from the dance revolution game and Francesca nudged Henry.

"Let's play Dance Revolution."

The music played as they stepped. By the fifth song, they were exhausted. Casey finished playing the shooting game and dared Henry to dance one last song with her. Henry had a high energy level, as boys often do. He was doing fine until the last 60 seconds. Vomit spewed out of his mouth as if he was going through an exorcism. His bile covered the screen of the game. The people around them screwed up their faces. The last she knew, vomiting wasn't a new phenomenon.

"I'll go tell the waiter," Francesca scurried off.

"Are you okay Henry?" Casey asked.

"Yes, but I'm going to sit down," Henry said.

Everyone who noticed what happened looked at them. Casey rolled her eyes at them.

"Come on Henry, let's go find dad."

They went back to their table; Adam was on his second round of dessert.

"Do you two want anything else?"

"Nah, I'm full."

"Where's Francesca?"

"She went to get something." Casey did not intend to tell her dad that Henry had redecorated the Dance Revolution game. Telling her dad would make him less likely to let Henry do what kids do best, play. Francesca came to the table and sat next to Casey while Henry sat next to Adam.

"Are you guys ready to go?" Adam asked.

"Yeah, I've had enough fun to last me a few days," Casey said. They had their fair share of food and fun. Adam paid their bill and they left the table. They tried to navigate the walkway but patrons continued to pour inside D & B and it proved to be a daunting task.

CHAPTER TWENTY

Francesca and Casey sat on a bench in the courtyard. The wind was mischievous today. Some of the girls tried to hold their skirts down, while others allowed their skirts to fly above their waist. It was a happy day for teenage boys.

Francesca shook her head.

"If this was a video game, you'd need a parent to make the purchase," Casey said laughing.

"Have you replaced your shoes yet?" Francesca asked.

"Nope! I'm pissed off. I wish I never went to Killer Shoes that day!"

"I told you, Sissy can hook you up!"

"Okay, give me her number."

"Give me your phone. I'll put in the number." Francesca entered the number and gave Casey the phone.

"Give her a call. The prom will be here before you know it." Francesca was right; Casey tried to put off the inevitable.

"I'll give her a call."

Nu joined them in the courtyard. Francesca got restless. Casey didn't blame her. If she had a boyfriend, she wouldn't want him to watch the peep show either.

"Let's go inside." Francesca didn't wait for a response. She held Nu's hand and he followed whether he wanted to or not.

"Do you have your suit for the dance?" Francesca asked.

"Don't worry. I'll have it in time for the dance."

"I can't wait to see what you'll be wearing." His face beamed.

"But you'll have to wait!" Francesca enjoyed teasing Nu. He took it well.

"Come here," Nu looked into her eyes. "You're so beautiful."

The level of entertainment heightened when the assistant principal's briefcase flew open; it created a ticker tape effect. A few pages made their way over to where Casey sat in the courtyard. The assistant principal looked like a swooping bird as he ran back and forth to retrieve the documents. Out of the corner of her eye, Casey saw Sissy walking on the lawn so she got up and walked quickly toward her.

"Sissy," she shouted. The weather was changing quickly and the wind got fiercer by the second. Sissy walked to the parking lot. Casey followed her. Sissy walked up to a man who got out of the passenger side of a red Dodge Charger. She stopped in front of him. Sissy giggled, tossed her hair and twirled her curls around her index finger. The wind pulled the tail of Casey's jacket away from her body when her cell phone beeped. She stopped and retrieved the message. Casey looked up after she read the message.

He held Sissy's hand. Casey stopped and walked backwards before she turned around. Her breathing slowed and she went back to the bench.

A flash of red zipped by when the Dodge Charger drove out of the circle. Sissy walked back through the courtyard. Casey ran over to catch up with her.

"Hey, Sissy!"

Sissy stopped and looked in Casey's direction. Casey was out of breath by the time she got to Sissy.

"What's your name again?"

"Casey. Francesca said you could hook me up with a deal on a nice pair of shoes."

"Sure, I can set that up for you. When do you want to do it?"

"Sooner than later. I'm running out of time," Casey said.

"I'll give you my number. Saturday is a good day if you're free." Casey went into the building. She saw Francesca and Nu in the hall.

She approached Francesca. "I'm meeting Sissy on Saturday."

"I hope you find something you like," Francesca said.

"I have a test to take. See you later."

Casey traveled down the hall to class. After studying all weekend, when she saw the test, everything she studied faded into her nonexistent memory. There's nothing more maddening than having the answer right at the tip of your temporal lobes and not be able to access it.

Her face reddened under the pressure and time quickly ran out. When she handed in her test, it had her name and an impressive array of drawings minus the answers to the questions. The test was a blur. Casey was upset with her performance, but there would be another test next week. *I'll do better*.

Casey was looking forward to getting a replacement shoes. She looked out the bus window; she was traveling to an undesirable part of town. When she arrived, no one else was there. Casey sat on a bench in Wilkinson Park on the north side of town. It wasn't a place Casey frequented, but she'd heard about it from students at school. 'Anything goes in Wilkinson Park' was the rumor. It was a place where teens drank and engaged in other questionable activities. Casey suggested that they meet elsewhere, but Sissy insisted that they meet at the park. When she looked at her watch, it was 10 AM. It was humid and the back of her shirt clung to her wet back. Sissy showed up minutes later.

"Sorry I'm late. I missed the bus and the next one came 10 minutes later."

Casey exhaled, "I was starting to get worried. Have you heard from your contact?"

"Yes, he will be here any minute."

They looked at one another awkwardly before looking around the deserted park. His weight crushed dried leaves, and twigs snapped as he approached them. It reminded her of a weird dream she had when she was a child. In the dream, she was in a park on a merry-go-round when a large animal ran toward her. She got off the merry-go-round and ran. A tiger chased her through the park until she arrived at a cliff. An endless fall ensued and she woke up screaming. The heavy scent of nicotine surrounded them.

"Let's do this!" A deep baritone voice spoke from behind them. He towered six feet into the air, with slick dark brown hair, a crooked nose and green eyes. The sun was hot, yet he wore black. His pants put bell-bottoms to shame. Chains hung from silver hoops sewn into the fabric like masochist lace.

Sissy turned around. "Hi, Tulip. This is the girl I told you about."

His eyes traveled up and down Casey's frame.

"Okay! So what type of shoe are you looking for?"

"It's hard to say. I will know it when I see it."

Tulip pulled a book out he had tucked in the back of his pants. Casey and Sissy looked at one another before their eyes returned to him.

"Here, have a look. Let me know if you see anything you like."

He pulled out a cigarette and lit it with a skull lighter. He let go a puff of smoke in their direction. Casey coughed as the smoke hugged her face. His hands were huge and he had the hairiest forearm she had ever seen. She flipped through his vast collection of shoes. It was mind numbing; each shoe was more beautiful than the one before.

"I need to sit down. There's a lot to go through." Casey was happy to get away from the heavy nicotine odor building around them. Sissy didn't seem to mind. She walked to a merry-go-round nearby and sat down on the base while Sissy and Tulip chatted. His lips hugged the cigarette affectionately before he passed it to Sissy who equally shared the enthusiasm.

"There's a few of them I like. What's your asking price?"

Tulip spit and clenched the tip of his chin, "One hundred seventy-five to three-hundred seventy-five dollars."

Casey let the price simmer in her head for a moment. She stood up and showed him a shoe in the folder.

"This is as close as it will get to what I'm looking for."

"You don't look happy with your choice. I'll have a new shipment in a few days."

"I'll get that one but I'm short on funds. I'll have the money next week!"

Tulip waved his head. "I don't hold shoes! Money talks." He rubbed his thumb against the other fingers.

Casey's face soured.

"You know what, I'll make an exception." Sissy moved closer, Tulip grasped the side of her hip. He looked at Sissy. "What do you think?" Sissy shrugged her shoulders.

"Give her a chance."

"It's settled then. When you get the money, we'll do the transaction!"

"I'm glad we have that settled. I have to go. Are you coming Sissy?" Casey asked.

Sissy leaned in closer to Tulip. "No. I'm going to hang out here for a while."

"Okay, I'll see you later."

Casey walked away towards the entrance of the park to the bus stop. A loud hum resounded as the bus approached. She had arrived at the bus stop just in time. In a hot second, she was gone.

Casey laid on her bed and stared as the ceiling fan spun. The haze the blades created as it intermingled with the air hypnotized her but it was interrupted by an atrocious odor that tickled her nose. Out of the corner of her eye, she saw Randy.

"Shoo, Randy! Naughty boy!" Henry waltzed in and flopped down on her bed.

"Get out Randy!" Henry said. Randy wobbled out of the room. "What's wrong Casey?"

"Nothing." She dragged the word.

"I'm taking Randy for a walk. Do you want to come?"

"Nah, I'm not in the mood."

"Come on Casey. It'll be fun," he tugged at her hand. "All right all right. I'll get dressed."

Henry left the room and went downstairs. Casey went down a few minutes later.

"Where are mom and dad?" asked Casey. "I don't know," said Henry. "When I woke up they weren't here."

"Okay then. Let's go."

They entered the park. The sky was cloudy, marring an otherwise beautiful day. Casey let Henry roam a bit, but not too far from her eyesight. Randy sniffed the grass, his tail straightening when he found something edible. Henry tossed a ball and Randy brought the ball back to him. As they continued their exchange, it brought them closer to the pond. Casey walked to a tree near the pond and sat on a large rock. She looked out at the murky waters. Ducks floated on the pond and quacked occasionally. Randy jumped on top of the rocks at the edge of the pond and barked at the ducks. His barks rattled their serene environment and the ducks went airborne briefly before they landed on the other side.

"Daddy, I want to play." A man held a fishing rod and stood next to his son under the gazebo at the edge of the pond.

"Not now!"

"I wanna go play, Daddy."

Numbing echoes of cicadas hummed from the trees. Birds chirped here and there. Henry sat on a rock as Randy panted at the still water and whined.

"No, Randy you can't drink that. It will make you sick."

"I want to touch the water daddy!" The boy walked away and walked closer to the edge of the pond where Henry and Randy sat.

"Jeremy, get over here!"

"No! I want to fish in the water."

Jeremy tinkered on the edge of the rocks. He skipped from one rock to another. Casey got up and hurried over to where Henry was.

"Get over here!" Jeremy turned around and went back to his father.

"I've had enough Henry. Let's go."

Casey heart raced. She swore Jeremy was going to throw himself in the water before his dad screamed at him. She held Henry's hand and they walked away from the pond. Randy was hesitant at first but once he saw a flock of ducks sleeping on the grass ahead he hastened his pace. The last thing she heard when they reached the entrance of the park was… "Jeremy!"

CHAPTER TWENTY ONE

Casey noticed Mr. Reinhold's vintage car parked out front. She often got there before he did. When Casey saw his car, she hastened her steps and entered the office. A conversation was in full swing and his door was ajar. A beautiful, leggy, chocolate sister in a short dress gave Mr. Reinhold the run down. She slammed a pack of letters on his desk, and glared at him.

"What are you going to do with these? My bills need your attention." She threw her hands in the air. The bracelets cascaded and chimed as they hit one another when she scratched at the air like a cat.

"Come on Tina." He moved in closer, held her hands and brought them down to her side. Mr. Reinhold saw Casey in the background. Her eyes widened when she saw him and she hurried to her desk.

"Relax! We can talk about this later," he said.

"Can't a good woman walk in here and get what she wants?" She didn't wait for him to respond. Tina thrust herself unto him and kissed him, but his lips didn't reciprocate. She tossed some files on the floor that he had on his desk. The files cascaded to the floor. Tina paused and looked at him.

"I'm all laid out! Do you want this?" She molded her body in a hand gesture.

"I do, but not when you're acting crazy."

Casey took out her cell phone and made a call. The office phone rang and she answered.

"Mr. Reinhold, you have a call on line one." Casey spoke in an elevated tone.

Tina grabbed her bills, tucked them in her *Pucci* bag, and stormed out. Mr. Reinhold let out a heavy sigh.

"Hello, Reinhold Detective Agency."

"It's me. I thought you needed an escape hatch."

"Thank You." He hung up the phone and closed his office door.

Mr. Reinhold didn't discriminate when it came to women. He liked them in all shapes and races. Clearly, there were few dull moments at the office. In fact, Tina looked familiar. Casey searched her memory to place Tina's face. *I remember her! She's the woman who keyed her husband's car when she found out he cheated on her.* You would think Mr. Reinhold would be scared to venture down that road, but he wasn't.

He didn't come out of his office until closing time. His shame needed time to recuperate before it crawled back into the bowels of his ego. Casey couldn't help but laugh once she calmed down. Drama seemed to follow Mr. Reinhold wherever he went and if he wasn't careful, his extracurricular activities could hurt his business.

CHAPTER TWENTY TWO

When Casey got her paycheck, she felt like she was playing a game of hot potato. She couldn't wait to cash her check before it burned a hole in her palm. Once she got the money squared away, she contacted Sissy to set up the transaction. Tulip suggested dropping it off at school. Casey agreed and waited in front of her school underneath the gargantuan tree. Her hair fluttered as the wind fingered the strands of her hair. She saw Tulip pull up. He got out of the car and walked up to her with a gift bag in hand.

"Do you have the money?"
Casey took out a wad of cash and gave it to him. He counted it and handed her the bag.

"It was nice doing business with you."

"Likewise!" she said and they both went in opposite directions. Tulip got in his car and drove off.

A block away, two men sat in a car and observed the transaction that took place between them. Tim Paulson turned to his partner, "We need to keep a close eye on him."

Wilson scoffed, "Don't worry. If he's involved, we'll connect the dots."
Carl zoomed in with his sophisticated binoculars.

"She looks familiar." Carl tried to remember where he saw her.

"She's the girl from the park." Wilson looked at Carl while he chewed on a toothpick.

"Yeah. She left on the bus."

"Do you think she's involved?"

"She's obviously a customer, but we have bigger fish to fry." They followed Tulip's car at a safe distance.

CHAPTER TWENTY THREE

Everyone was talking about the prom and whether they were going or not. Francesca and Nu were ready for the dance. On the other hand, Casey wasn't ready. She stood in front of the mirror, held her prom dress against her body and lowered her eyes to the shoes on her feet. *They'd have to do*, whether she liked it or not! The shoes and dress looked nice together but nothing came close to the splendor of the first shoes.

What was equally saddening was that she was going solo to the dance. She scoffed and hung the dress in the closet. A heavy knock echoed from her bedroom door.

"Come in dad."

Adam stuck his head in. "How's it going?"

"Okay. Do you need anything?" Casey asked.

"No. I wanted to make sure you were okay." He entered the room and sat at the end of her bed. "Detective Ramos called earlier. He has a few questions for you."

Casey sulked. "I hope they catch them." Adam put his arms around her shoulder.

"Don't worry they'll get them."

"The principal of your school called me the other day..."

"Did I do something wrong?"

"No. He asked if I was interested in being a part of their vocational program. At first I said, 'I don't have enough hours in the day to complete the jobs I already have,' but he was very convincing. I accepted and I'll be working with vocational students who are interested in the construction field."

"I think that's great, Dad!"

Adam was surprised. Teenagers didn't like it when their parents worked at their school.

"A few students will be working with my company on light jobs."

"Yes. It will be nice to have you close. Besides, I'm the same person no matter where I am." She smiled.

He hugged her and kissed her on the side of her head. "I'll let you get back to what you were doing."

CHAPTER TWENTY FOUR

I swear, if Clarissa doesn't stop kicking the back of my shoe, I'm going to take it off and slap her with it. I hope it has dog poo or a fresh gooey substance on the bottom to redecorate her face. Casey looked over her shoulder and glared at her. Clarissa had a smug look on her doughy face. Hate was a strong word, but it was the only feeling that surfaced when Clarissa bugged her.

Every dog has its day and she hoped Clarissa would have hers soon. Casey would have to deal with her in their last period class. She wasn't looking forward to it, but she was looking forward to Mrs. Shepler's birthday party. She was a great teacher and all of her students knew it. She was four-foot nine-inches tall with straight black hair that hung past her waist. Mrs. Shepler looked like a younger pint size version of Cher. Any time a student got a complex math problem correct, Mrs. Shepler did the 'running man' dance.

The party was in full swing. They passed balloons around occasionally before they fell to the floor or a student popped them. The indistinguishable sound of chatter mingled with the music that played loud enough for them to hear, but low enough not to disturb the other classes in session.

Refreshments covered one of the tables and the other table was filled with junk food. Casey was having a good time but Clarissa kept staring at her. Casey rolled her eyes and turned away. Clarissa congregated with her crew as she drank heartily. Casey went over to the window. The sky was clear and the courtyard outside was filled with students. A tiny green lizard ran inside through a small gap in the window and rubbed against her hand.

Lizards were the least worrisome of creepy things. She didn't mind them at all. She remembered them fondly from her childhood. Though she was inside a brick fortress, when she saw the lizard, it brought her back to a time in her childhood. She could smell the wild grass and envision her skin grazed by tall itchy shrubs. Casey made a loop on a wild grass stem and slowly eased the loop around the lizard's neck; the loop tightened and she walked the lizard like a dog on a leash. On mischievous days, she'd twirl the lizard on the leash through the air and coined it, *The Flying Lizard Trapeze Act.*

Casey looked at Clarissa and sported a devilish grin. She picked the lizard up by the tail and put it in her shirt pocket. The lizard wiggled in her pocket. Casey walked over to the refreshment desk to get a soda.

"Bring me a coke please!" Clarissa shouted.

Oh no she didn't! I'm not her maid...but she said please.

Casey took a deep breath, picked up the coke and brought it over to Clarissa. She grabbed the coke out of Casey's hand and turned her back. She laughed hysterically with her comrades at Casey's expense. Casey bubbled with anger. She took the lizard out of her pocket, dropped it in the opening at the back of

Clarissa's collar and walked away. Within seconds, Clarissa screamed and undressed herself as if her clothes were on fire. Her boobs almost jumped out of her bra as she frantically clawed at her body. The boys in the class went nuts and sang, *"Extra! Naked! Take it off! Shabba…"*
Casey gained temporary satisfaction from Clarissa's humiliation.

Mrs. Shepler's eyes bulged. "What in the world is going on?"

"Something was crawling inside my shirt," she said in a whiney voice.

"Well, whatever it was it's gone now. Put your shirt on." Mrs. Shepler gave Clarissa her shirt.

"Alright calm down. This probably wasn't the first and it won't be the last time you'll see breasts." *Hopefully, this will be the last time this happens in my class*. The party continued, but there was an invisible elephant in the room and it made a fool of Clarissa.

CHAPTER TWENTY FIVE

"Are you any closer to getting the information I need?" Orli's impatience was visible on her face.

"I'm sorry, but my contacts went cold a few days ago." It was more like a week ago but he couldn't tell her that. In reality, his contacts outsmarted him. Once they got their first payment, they went *AWOL*. They strung him along for weeks and laughed all the way to the bank. Little did he know that he had an ally who was working on his behalf.

"If you solve this case, I will pay you a bonus." Orli had enough of Mr. Reinhold's ineffective methods. "I'm running out of patience, Thomas." She walked towards the front door, and paused. She turned around, went over to Casey's desk, and gave her a business card.

Later that evening, Casey contacted Orli. They agreed to meet at a café downtown.

"I'm not sure how much your boss told you, but I'll fill you in. I think my son may be living a double life. I hired your boss to look into his affairs. The company he keeps is an undesirable bunch."

Casey sat before her and listened attentively.

"I went into his room a few months ago and I found $10,000 in a shoe box under his bed. I'm a rich woman, but I don't give my son that kind of money. He works part time at one of my charities. I'm a firm believer in hard work. Nothing comes easy, and when it does, a criminal charge usually accompanies it."

"I need to know more about your son. Do you have a photo?"

"As a matter of fact I do." Orli took her wallet out of her Jimmy Choo handbag. "That's him." She gave Casey the picture.

"He doesn't look familiar. How old is he?"

"Nineteen. I need to know what he's up to. I'm not one of those delusional parents that swear that their child has never done anything wrong. I'll be the one to call the police if he breaks the law!"

It was clear Orli was serious and her emotions wouldn't hinder her from doing the right thing, even if it hurt.

CHAPTER TWENTY SIX

Instead of dreaming about what she would wear the next day, Casey dreamt she was buried in a pile of shoes. She woke up with cold sweat running across her forehead. A young man rose above Casey's windowsill. She screamed and the unnerving sound startled him. He lost his footing and fell to the ground. Her scream cut through the quiet house and echoed through the window. Her father ran up the staircase and opened her bedroom door.

"What's wrong?" Casey ran into her father's arms.

"There's a guy outside my window."
Adam walked over to the window.

"I'm sorry honey. I forgot to tell you that one of my vocational students would be cleaning the gutters today."

"I have to go and check on him." He kissed Casey's forehead and left the room.

Adam went outside. He saw Sean on the grass and the ladder was on the ground nearby.

"Damn it. I knew this teacher thing was a bad idea." Alan ran to him.

"Sean!" Alan shook him lightly. Sean moaned and his eyes fluttered. "Are you okay?"
Sean nodded his head.

"I think so." He sat up.

"I wasn't spying on her. I swear."

"Relax. No one is accusing you of anything." He gave Sean a hand and helped him to his feet.

"That was a dangerous fall; I'm taking you to the hospital."

"My mom's going to freak out."

"Don't worry, I'll talk to her."

They walked to his truck in the driveway and drove to the hospital. Adam spent a couple of hours at the hospital with Sean before he returned home.

"How's your student?" Casey walked through as Kelly asked.

"He has a minor bump, that's all."

"Everything is okay. I took him home and spoke to his parents."

CHAPTER TWENTY SEVEN

Francesca and Casey must have had an unconscious coordination while asleep. Both of their outfits were from the Vera Wang collection. Casey wore a black tank with silver embellishments, and black skinny jeans. While Francesca wore a pleated-black jeans skirt, a white tuxedo shirt accessorized with a black bow tie and a long pearl necklace. Her bushy curly hair flowed against her round face.

Sean mulled over what he'd say. Looking at Casey wouldn't make the task any easier. To say she was cute would be an understatement. She was gorgeous.

"Hi. I'm Sean." He extended his hand. "Sean Avery. I apologize for scaring you the other day. I didn't know Mr. Sullivan had a daughter." Casey managed a guarded smile.

"Apology accepted." She shook his hand. "You had a dangerous fall. Are you okay?" She felt bad that he fell because of her. She sighed and it lightened her mood.

"I'm okay. Thanks for asking."

"This is my best friend Francesca and her boyfriend Nu."

"Nice to meet you."

"Well, I have to go to class," he said as he walked away. Casey got a full view of his back profile.

"I could mold those buns into a cake," Casey said to Francesca and chuckled.

He turned hastily, "What?"

"Oh, nothing." Casey looked at Francesca and flexed her eyebrows, blushing.

Francesca was preoccupied, texting. She sensed that if she lit a match, it would ignite the tension between them.

"If you don't scoop him up someone else will! You know the mechanics of desire; no one will want him until you do."

Casey nodded her head in agreement.

"He's up for grabs. Latch on to him while you can."

"I'm not looking for a boyfriend." Francesca elbowed her.

"Who said anything about him being your boyfriend? It's a new era. Girls don't wait on guys to ask them out."

"Point taken! Now can you please move on to another topic?"

Francesca laughed, "Okay. I won't say another word."

Casey entered her room and the pale pink décor calmed her. The prom was a week away but the excitement she once harbored, fizzled at gunpoint when she was robbed at Killer Shoes. She walked over to the closet and opened the door. Her prom dress glistened amongst her other garments. Her dad poked his head in.

"Sean will be here tomorrow after school to finish cleaning the gutters. Try not to scare him," Adam said and smiled.

"Sure Dad." Casey smirked. Adam walked away and backtracked.

His head popped back in unexpectedly and Casey jumped.

"You scare too easily!"

"I can't help it dad. Ever since the robbery, I've been a bit skittish."

"You'll get over it in time. Anyway, I think you have an admirer."

"Sean's been asking a lot of questions about you."

Casey buried her head in her pillow. "Dad!"

"He's a good kid."

She removed the pillow once she heard his footsteps travel away from her room. She flopped her legs on the bed like a fish out of water and smiled.

Muffled chatter followed by a clambering was heard outside. Casey walked over to the window and pressed her nose against the glass. Sean and her dad were moving plywood from the back of his truck and Henry and Randy chased butterflies around the yard.

Adam's elevated voice traveled through the yard and he pointed toward the house. Randy's head lowered, he slowly walked inside. An active worksite was no place for kids. Henry wasn't particularly happy about the restrictions, but he knew failing to comply would result in a metamorphosis from an easy-going dad to a micro-managing father. Casey left her room and passed her mother in the hallway.

"Where are you off to?"

"I'm going to get a bite to eat."

"Keep an eye on your brother. I'm going to take a nap."

"Sure mom."

Casey looked over the railing as she walked down the staircase. Henry was watching cartoons and Randy was lying at his feet.

She went into the kitchen and opened the refrigerator. Casey reheated a slice of pizza and waited for it to cool. The pizza was gone in a few bites and she washed it down with a glass of water. The buzz of a chainsaw echoed through the kitchen. Casey went outside. It was a comfortable 70 degrees, ideal weather for working outdoors. Sean climbed up the ladder to clean the gutter. Adam use to do it until he hurt his back two years ago. After that, he got one of the workers to clean it. Casey looked at her father. Goggles protected his eyes. He measured a length of wood before lowering the lever of the table saw. Tiny remnants of wood shavings burst into the air before they landed on the ground.

Sean's body got lost in the light of the sun when he climbed up the ladder. The sunlight outlined his hair, which was short on the sides and modestly spiked on the top. He scooped debris from the gutter and dumped it in a small bucket. Clouds gathered around the sun and hogged its rays. When it resurfaced, his skin glistened, reflecting the sweat coming from his pores. He passed the back of his hand across his forehead to wipe away the perspiration.

Casey went inside and riffled through the pantry. She grabbed a bag of cookies, placed them on a plate, made a pitcher of lemonade and put them on a tray. She cautiously walked outside with the tray in her hands. The trees were still with the lack of a breeze, reminiscent of a painting, and the flutter of a butterfly interrupted the stillness. Her father was still cutting wood and Sean was on his way down the ladder. He took off his gloves and put them in his back pocket. A breeze picked up, and loose strands escaped Casey's braid when the wind played with her hair. For a moment, Sean felt entangled in her essence.

"Hi." All of Casey's front teeth were on display with her huge smile. Sean returned the smile.

"Dad, I brought you some refreshments. Where should I put them?"

"Thanks. I have a folding table in here somewhere. He rummaged around in the shed for a few moments before finding it. Here you can put it on this." He opened the table and she put the tray on it.

She poured a glass of lemonade for her dad and took it over to him.

"Thanks." Adam smiled and winked at her. She then gave Sean a glass.

"If you'd like to sit down, I can take you to the front porch," Casey suggested.

"Mr. Sullivan, I'm almost done with cleaning the gutters." Sean walked over to the table and took a few cookies. "Is it okay if I take a break?"

Adam laughed, "Technically, you're already on break. Go on."

Casey and Sean walked to the front of the house and opened the miniature gate that led to the porch. He exhaled, "it feels good to be off my feet."

"I can only imagine how achy you'll be tomorrow." Casey twirled her hair and wrapped it with the Scrunchie she was wearing on her wrist.

He smiled, and his dimples eclipsed his broad cheekbones. He had a ruggedness about him but his hands felt soft when they briefly touched hers.

"This is a nice neighborhood."

"Yes, but it can be too quiet sometimes and there aren't many teenagers around."

"That's a good thing. Where I live, there are too many teenagers. I can send a few your way." He chuckled.

"That's okay. I have a feeling I'd regret it if you did."

"School's almost over. I know a lot of students are excited about that," he said.

"Are you?" Casey asked.

"No. I spend my summers with my dad in Boston, but I'd rather stay here and get a summer job."

"Sounds like a good idea. Maybe you can convince your parents to agree on it," Casey suggested.

"It's worth the try but I have to get a job offer first."

"You have three weeks before school is over. You still have time to find something."

"I know, and the prom is almost here," he said.

"Are you going?" she asked.

"Yes, I can't wait." His cheerful spirit went somber.

"I'm going to have a blast...all by myself," Casey said.

He shook his head. "You're too beautiful to go to the prom alone."

"There's still time to change that." Casey sipped on the glass of lemonade with a slight smirk on her face.

"Will you go with me to the prom?" Sean's heart raced while he waited for her response.

"I'd love to."

CHAPTER TWENTY EIGHT

Casey walked over and sat next to Francesca in the courtyard. Casey sat there in silence and it was unusual. When they were together in the courtyard, they always had something to talk about. Francesca looked at Casey and wrinkled her eyebrows.

"Why are you grinning?" Francesca's words went right over Casey's head.

"Hello! Earth to Casey." Francesca waved her hand in front of her face.

"Where were you?"

"Right here. Where else would I be?" Casey said.

"I've been trying to get your attention for the past few minutes."

A surprised look came over her face. "Sorry about that." She reverted to grinning.

"There you go again with that silly grin."

"I can't help it. I'm happy."

"Are you going to tell me or am I going to have to pry it out of you?"

Casey laughed.

"That's not necessary, I'll tell you. Sean asked me to the prom."

Francesca's face relaxed. "That's awesome news. I'd be smiling too if he asked me. He is adorable."

"I know."

"Now that we've got that out of the way, how did your talk with Detective Ramos go?"

"Not so good. He blew me off. My assumptions weren't worth chasing!" She was miffed.

"Knowing you, you're going to pursue it anyway." Francesca looked at Casey out of the corner of her eye.

Casey scoffed. "Yup."

While the client in Mr. Reinhold's office kept him busy, Casey went through Mrs. Rothman's file. There was a photo of each of his informants attached to their information, along with any intelligence they provided. The surveillance photos taken by one of his operatives provided the only useful information. The man from the arcade was in one of the photos. Things were starting to make sense.

Deep down, she felt she had the pieces of information to help solve Orli's case. She looked at the surveillance photos. *I'm missing something. What or who connects Orli to the man in the photo?*

Casey called Mr. Reinhold's extension.

"Is it okay if I take a fifteen minute break?"

"Sure," he agreed.

She went outside the office and called Francesca.

"I need your advice," Casey said.

"What's wrong?"

Casey exhaled, "Okay. Remember the case I told you about?"

"Yes. What's going on?"

"I think Tulip's selling stolen goods out of a location without signage displayed."

"A hunch isn't enough." Francesca tried to reason with her.

"Wait…there's more. Do you remember the guy Sissy set me up with to buy the shoes?"

"Yes."

"If he's involved, I can get in trouble for buying stolen merchandise."

It was dead quiet for a few minutes. Francesca broke the silence. "Don't you think you're your imagination has gone overboard?"

"No. I think I'm onto something."

"Businesses don't always advertise their warehouse locations so they can minimize theft." Francesca tried to find a reasonable explanation, but Casey's theory made sense.

"Okay, but you need more to go on before you go back to the police," Francesca advised.

"Yeah, I know. I have to get back to work. I'll talk to you later."

When Casey got back inside the office, she put Orli's file in her bag. *He won't miss it and I'll have it back before he knows it's gone.* When she got home from work, her family had already eaten dinner. Casey thought about what Francesca said while she ate alone in the kitchen. When she was done, she washed her dishes and went upstairs. She turned on the faucet to prepare for a long hot bath. Soaking in the hot tub helped her to relax and clear her mind.

Casey was a prune by the time she got out and wrapped her body in a terry robe. The background noise from the TV in her parent's room trickled down the hall. Henry's door was open but the lights were off. Casey went into her room, dressed and laid sideways on the bed, falling asleep. For the first hour, she slept well, but her sleep digressed into bad dreams. Casey relived the robbery at Killer Shoes. She once again felt the emotions, smelled the odor in the room, and heard the voices of the robbers. It was strange. Casey second-guessed herself in the dream. She looked at the robbers and heard their voices. She suddenly woke up and threw the sheets aside, looking at the time, *4:00 AM*. Casey lay back on the bed and closed her eyes. A few minutes later, she jumped up, her eyes wide cupping her hands over her mouth. She had an A-HA moment. The pieces of the case were coming together but she would have to wait until after school before she could do anything about it.

It took a while, but she managed to go back to sleep. The sound of her alarm clock made her drag her eyelids open. Casey looked at the time, 6:30 AM. She turned over, hit the snooze button, and went back to sleep. The snooze button rang fifteen minutes later, but this time she didn't wake up. At 6:50, her father walked inside her room.

"Aren't you going to school?" he asked. Casey jumped up and looked at the time.

"Yes!" She tossed the covers off and climbed out of the bed.

He shook his head. "You're going to make me late," he mumbled.

Casey put on her clothes, brushed her teeth and rushed downstairs.

"That was quick."

"I don't want to be late." Casey tossed her bag over her shoulder. Henry gave her a peculiar glance.

"Are you going to school looking like that?"

Casey had on a purple lace top, black wedge shoes and her pajama pants.

"Yikes." She ran upstairs, put on black skinny jeans, and ran back downstairs.

"All right, let's go," Adam said.

"Thanks Henry." Casey kissed him on the cheek.

During lunch, Francesca and Casey met up in the courtyard. Nu joined them shortly after.

"I had the weirdest dream last night. I relived the entire robbery."

"That must have been scary."

"It was scary, but I think I'm a bit closer to the truth."

"Good for you. You'll feel better once you solve this case. I can't wait for the old Casey to return."

"Have I been that bad?"

"Yes. You've lost yourself."

"I'm sorry." Casey lowered her head.

"You won't understand unless you've experienced it."

Sean walked up from behind her.

"Hi. How are you?" She looked to her side and forced a smile.

"Okay." An awkward silence fell between them.

"What's wrong?"

"It's nothing. I have some stuff to sort out." Casey made light of her troubling situation.

"All right then. I'll catch you later," he said and walked away.

"Are you trying to get rid of him?"

"No. I'm trying to make sense of something that makes no sense."

"Well, you had better hurry up before he thinks you're not interested."

"You're nuts Francesca. I'm already going to the dance with him."

"I'm not talking about the dance. Did you see the way he looked at you? The dance is only one evening. He wants to be your shadow." Francesca giggled and winked at her.

Casey smiled. "Maybe so, but I'm preoccupied right now. I have a meeting with Orli, I need her to clarify a few things for me."

Mr. Reinhold went out for lunch, so Mrs. Rothman agreed to come in a half-hour before her appointment with him to talk with Casey. Casey looked through her file.

"What are your children's names?"

"John and Ressa, why?"

"No particular reason. Do you have a recent picture of them?"

"I have a picture of my son and an old primary school photo of my daughter." She looked through her wallet and showed Casey the photo of her daughter. The girl looked familiar but Casey couldn't put her finger on it.

"Can I hold on to this for a few days?"

"Sure, but I want it back in mint condition."

"So…have you found out anything?" Orli questioned.

"Actually, I have, but I can't prove it yet."

Orli's eyebrows rose. "Keep digging."

Orli looked at her watch, got up and walked over to the window.

"Your boss is here."

Mr. Reinhold rambled on about useless information. Orli yawned and stood up. She was tired of his recycled information.

"I have a ceremony to attend later on this evening so I have to leave now." She got up and walked out of his office.

CHAPTER TWENTY NINE

Mrs. Shepler stood with her back to the class and wrote a math problem on the board. She explained each step. Casey jotted down the problem and tried to work it out. Math only made sense when the answer made sense. Suddenly, a light bulb went off in Casey's head.

A thumping vibrated through her chair. Casey clenched her eyes, and her cheeks flushed red. She paced her breath to calm her nerves. A harder thump caused the chair to slide. Other students heard the noise and looked in her direction. Casey turned and looked at Clarissa and froze. She turned back around.

Seconds later a devilish grin spread across her face. School couldn't finish fast enough. When the bell rang, she raced to the front of the building to meet Francesca. She was out of breath by the time she reached her.

Casey exhaled. "I have to go downtown to the precinct."

"For what?"

"I can't explain now. I have to call Orli and let her know."

It was hard to give someone news that would change their picturesque life. But Orli was a tough woman. She listened as Casey poured out the news to her and encouraged her to go to the police with the information she had just told her.

Nu offered to take her downtown and Francesca tagged along.

Detective Ramos was nestled in a comfortable chair when another officer summoned him.

"To what do I owe the pleasure?"

"I have new information about the robbery, Casey started out. The robber's voices were mechanical, and the padded body armor they wore distorted their figures. They made every effort to disguise themselves."

"Now we're getting somewhere." His gaze was intense when he heard the new development. "Is there anything else?"

"John Rothman is involved. Actually, I bought a pair of shoes from him. He goes by the name of Tulip." Casey hadn't recognized him in the picture Orli showed her before. "He was dressed as a Goth when I met him. He may be involved in a theft ring selling merchandise out of an unmarked warehouse on Houston Street."

"And you know this how?"

"I saw a picture of the warehouse in a few of the surveillance photos from a case file my boss is working on," Casey admitted.

"Does anyone else know about this?"

"His mother, Orli Rothman."

He picked up the phone. "What's her number?"

Casey gave him the number. The phone rang incessantly before it disconnected.

"She did mention she had to prepare for a ceremony this evening."

"Do you recall where?"

"No. She didn't say where."

Orli waited until John left. She went into his room and searched though his draws. She found a pack of condoms and cigarettes. She moved on to his closet. Orli looked through the pockets of his clothing. She used a plastic step stool to reach the top shelf of the closet. Stacks of Playboy magazines, comic books, and baseball hats in every color known to man lined a portion of the shelf. She tried to put things back exactly as they were so he wouldn't know she was there. In the left corner on the top shelf were Nike shoeboxes and she looked through them. She found a box filled with money. Orli exhaled before she opened another box, which contained three nine-millimeter weapons. Her jaw clenched and her heart raced. She closed the box and looked inside the last box in the corner. Sophisticated voice-altering headsets were inside. Her heart ached. She put the boxes back in order, stepped down from the ladder and turned around.

Her eyes widened when John stared back at her.

"I wish you hadn't seen that."

He walked over to her, grabbed her by the arm and threw her on the bed.

"I forgot something and came back to get it. I'm glad I did or you'd have time to rat me out to the police."

Orli tried to compose herself. "I don't care what you've done. We can fix this."

"Oh please! Don't waste your breath. The last thing you want is for your perfect name to be dragged through the mud."

"That's not true. I love you John; don't make the situation any worse."

"Shut up!"

He put his hand in the back of his pants and pulled out a gun. "Don't try anything." Cruel laughter escaped his lips followed by an evil grin.

He went to the closet, keeping the gun pointed at her. Orli's eyes were primed on the muzzle. He grabbed the money and put it in a backpack.

"Don't feel bad. You were a good mother, but adopting me didn't change what I'd endured before you came along." He waved the gun at her as he continued to fill the bag with money. Orli's eyes followed his every move.

"Please don't do this. I can get you the best lawyers to get you out of this mess you've gotten yourself into."

"You can't help me this time, Mom. I'm sorry about this." He zipped up the bag, tossed it over his shoulder and walked backwards out of the room. When he got to the staircase, he turned around and ran down the stairs. Orli got up and ran down the hall to her room, grabbed her purse and ran barefoot after him. She closed in on him just outside the front door.

"John, STOP!" Orli shouted in a breathy voice.

He continued to walk swiftly down the entrance steps and she pursued him. A crackling sound pierced the air and John fell to the ground. He twitched as electrical pulses traveled throughout his body.

"9-1-1…what's your emergency?"

"There's a domestic disturbance at 1720 Patience Lane."

The police got there within five minutes, cuffed and arrested John.

Detective Ramos arrived on the scene. "I tried to reach you earlier." He wanted to discourage her from doing anything that could spook her son but he was too late.

"Yes, I saw the missed calls after I called the police. There are a few things in my son's closet that may be of interest to you."

He shook his head. "Okay, I'll have a look. I'm sorry about your son."

"Thank you."

Carl and Tim arrived as Detective Ramos was about to go inside Orli's residence. Agent Paulson approached the officer, while Agent Wilson, a stout man with thinning hair and a baby face, stood outside their tinted vehicle. His stomach slouched over his pants and the buttons on his shirt strained to keep the shirt together. Carl displayed his FBI badge.

"Agent Paulson, FBI." Carl looked down at the officer as he stroked the patch of hair on his chin.

"I'm Detective Ramos. What can I do for you gentleman?"

"For starters, you can hand over John Rothman. We have had him under surveillance for the past six months."

"I'll be happy to do so after I'm done with him."

"I could easily pull rank on you, but I'm a reasonable man," Paulson said, and gave Detective Ramos a business card.

Three days later, Casey sat and watched *Jurassic Park*, a movie she turned to when she was bored tremendously. She watched dinosaurs chase their snacks around a jungle and it always made her laugh. Casey paused the movie and switched to the TV guide channel to see if anything good would be on. A breaking news segment interrupted the screen.

"Good evening. I'm Channing Taylor, reporting from the Ninth precinct. We have an update on the string of robberies that have been taking place around town.

The police department has apprehended five suspects who were a part of a sophisticated theft operation. We have just learned that John Rothman, Dietrich Rom and three Central High School students were arrested for their alleged involvement in a string of robberies around town."

John Rothman and Dietrich Rom's mug shots displayed on the screen. Casey recognized Dietrich as the man she saw at D & B.

"We will keep you up to date with additional information once it becomes available.

I'm Channing Taylor reporting for Channel Seven News."

The phone rang and Casey answered.

"It looks like your snooping paid off. I just saw your handy work on the news."

Casey laughed. "Yeah, I was just watching."

"I am glad it's over. Now we can focus on our stuff. Are we still on for tomorrow?"

"Yes, we'll get ready from my house."

"Oh by the way, I've reserved a limousine to pick us up."

Francesca almost deafened Casey with her squeals. Casey laughed, "Relax it's just a limo, not a ride to the afterlife."

"Are you going to pick up Sean or will he meet you there?"

"We're picking him up."

CHAPTER THIRTY

Casey was questioned at the Ninth Precinct. When the police were finished, the FBI had their turn. She cooperated fully, and during the process she found out information the public didn't know. Initially, the FBI got a tip about a sophisticated theft ring. Through further investigation, they discovered that Dietrich Rom and John Rothman dabbled in selling assault weapons. Once the FBI got a search warrant to search the warehouse, they found thirty crates of military-grade weapons, Kevlar vests and other tactical gear. In addition, John's DNA matched the sexual assault case that took place at Claire's Boutique.

Once he was officially charged, Orli met with Mr. Reinhold to settle her payment. Orli had some leeway in the matter. She managed to broker a deal with Mr. Reinhold and it involved Casey getting sixty-percent of the payment from the case. After all, her efforts led to his arrest. Mr. Reinhold wasn't happy about the agreement, but Orli left him no choice. It was her way or no way.

The deal also forced him to make tough decisions to settle his debt. He put his beloved 1955 silver Mercedes Benz 190SL Cabrio convertible up for auction. When it was over, he was able to pay off Buddy. Mr. Reinhold was left with forty dollars from the sale of the car. It's hard to gauge if he learned anything from his experience. He was a creature of habit, and habits are hard to break.

Going to school was a ritual she couldn't escape. Rumors swirled and everyone was curious. They were anxious to find out which students were involved in criminal activity. Casey was clueless and so was everyone else. Orli called during her lunch hour. She gave Casey an earful of information, and by the end of the conversation, all of her questions were answered.

It made sense now; the picture Orli showed her weeks ago was of Clarissa. When Orli first met her and asked Clarissa what her name was, she couldn't pronounce her name and said 'Reesa.' Ever since then Orli had called her Reesa. Casey couldn't believe what she learned. Clarissa, Brandy and Lauren were charged with the robbery that took place at Killer Shoes and Orli confirmed that *Tulip* was John's street name.

Casey already knew that Dietrich Rom was the head of their crime ring but it turned out Dietrich was the man she saw at the arcade. He was also the owner of the warehouse. Dietrich used his legitimate carpet business as a front. He kept the stolen merchandise in the warehouse. Casey was glad that Clarissa was out of the picture, but not like this. She felt bad for Orli.

"Are you okay?" Francesca asked.

"Yeah," she said hesitantly.

"Clarissa, Lauren and Brandy were arrested."

"She was a troublesome witch." Francesca fumed.

"Well, it's over! I can move on now. I'll see you later at the house around five PM," Casey said.

"Absolutely," Francesca hugged Casey. She went to her last class before school finished. For the next forty-five minutes, much of what was said in class floated over her. The only thing that mattered was the sound of the bell. Once it rang, students bolted out of class like bulls chasing red capes.

When Casey arrived home, she saw a squad car parked in her driveway. Her dad stood outside with Detective Ramos and Casey walked over to them.

"Hi Dad, what's going on?"

"I came by to get the shoes you purchased from Tulip. They are stolen merchandise," said Detective Ramos.

"But…"

"Casey, get the shoes," Adam said.

She went inside, returned with the shoes and gave them to Detective Ramos.

Casey hugged her dad, silent tears flowing down her cheeks. She buried her head in his chest.

"It wasn't easy, but I managed to make it happen. I know how important it was to you."

Casey turned and looked at the detective. He went into his cruiser, took out a box and gave it to her. She opened it and sobbed.

"My shoes. You found my shoes." She wiped the tears from her eyes and hugged the detective. "Thank you."

"You're welcome." Detective Ramos smiled briefly.

"You have a future police officer on your hands," he said to her dad and got in the car.

Casey smiled and her tense limbs relaxed.

"I don't doubt that," said Adam. "Take care."

Detective Ramos waved and drove away.

The limousine pulled up in front of Casey's house and traveled to Nu's house. He looked handsome as he stepped into the glare of the streetlight. Francesca's eyes lit up when she saw him adorned in a steel-color suit with subtle glitter undertones and accentuated with a baby blue tie. The chauffeur got out and opened the door for him. Nu entered saying, "Good evening ladies. Are you ready to dance the night away?"

Francesca and Casey giggled, "But of course," Francesca replied in a faux English accent. Casey shook her head and smiled.

"One more stop." Casey's stomach fluttered. Sean peeked out of the window as the limo came to a stop, and quickly walked outside.

Casey's heartbeat quickened with each step that brought him closer. Sean stood out in the dimly lit street wearing a dapper white tuxedo with a pink tie, and a silk handkerchief in the breast pocket. Her nerves calmed and she gave herself permission to enjoy whatever the night had in store for her. In the blink of an eye, he was tangible. His lips planted a kiss on the back of her hand.

The limousine ride to the prom was short. The chauffeur got out and opened the door. The only thing missing was a red carpet. Nu and Francesca stepped out first. The first thing that caught his attention was Francesca's shoes as the light hit them and his eyes continued to rise. The four-inch glitterati heels gave adage to her modelesque stature. Nu's eyes traveled up the edge of her disco ball inspired mini-dress and to her smooth toffee-colored skin. His heart felt like it stopped and quickened all at once. Francesca had straightened her hair, and it trickled off her shoulders like a sheet of motionless dark water.

"You look beautiful." He looked up at the sky and fixed his tie.

Sean stepped out and extended his hand; Casey grasped it and stepped out. The chauffeur closed the door, returned to his seat, and drove away. They stepped up on the sidewalk. The whole time, her eyes never left him.

"You look..." Casey couldn't find the words to finish.

Sean smiled, "Thank You." Her expression said it all.

He raised their hands and twirled her. A gold necklace with fuchsia and pale pink gems hugged her neck. The fuchsia tiered dress draped her slender frame. A side ruche created a pleat effect that cascaded down to her ankles and a pale pink pearl accent clutch completed her look. Casey looked down at her feet and the pale pink shoes with satin roses and pink cubic zirconium in the center with glass heels, and clicked her heels. Unbridled joy ran through her veins.

Her long lustrous black hair curled away from her face and highlighted her green eyes. "You look stunning."

Casey blushed, "Thank you."

"Let's go inside." Casey wrapped her hand around his forearm and they entered the gymnasium.

There was no shortage of students there when they arrived. The music was in full swing and no one stood lining the walls. Students relaxed on the bleachers when their bodies got too hot. The principal stood as an armed guard all night over the punch. When he needed a break, the assistant principal took his place. There was no way anyone could spike the punch. Yet, by the looks of it, a few students had tipped the bottle before they got to the prom. Casey stood with Sean on the sidelines and they danced when she favored a song. She spotted Francesca slow jamming with Nu. Her Asian Hottie sure knew how to move on the dance floor.

She looked so happy. *I wish they sold happiness in a bottle. I'd invest in it; we all should.* Casey was a different kind of happy than she had ever been in her life. She was content to be there with Sean. No one looked at his or her watches. It was their night to let the hair down and dance the angst away. The last song to send them on their way was *"Time"* by the Black Eye Peas.

I had the time of my life and I owe it all to you, you y-y-y-y-y-y-y-y dirty bit!

The students when crazy when the beat morphed into a techno frenzy. They went into full geek mode and no technique was involved in their dance moves. All they had to do was keep moving. The students looked like beautiful zombies on an adrenaline high and for a moment, everything stood frozen in time. Everyone was well dressed in fabulous clothing and killer shoes.